STEVIE SMITH

was born in Hull in 1902, but when she was three she moved with her parents and sister to Avondale Road in Palmers Green – an address now immortalised in her own writings, the recent Hugh Whitmore stage play, *Stevie*, and its highly acclaimed film version, starring Glenda Jackson. Here she stayed for over sixty years, after her parents' death living with and devoted to her beloved 'Lion Aunt'.

Born Florence Margaret, nicknamed Stevie after Steve Donoghue the jockey, she went to Palmers Green High School and the North London Collegiate School for Girls and worked until retirement as private secretary to Sir George Newnes and Sir Neville Pearson, the magazine publishers. She first attempted to publish her poems in 1935 but was told to 'go away and write a novel'. *Novel On Yellow Paper* (1936) was the result. This and her first volume of poems, *A Good Time Was Had By All* (1937), established her reputation as a unique poetic talent and she published seven more collections, many of them illustrated by her own drawings. An accomplished and very popular reciter of her verse, both on the radio and at poetry readings, she won the Cholmondeley Award for Poetry and, in 1969, the Queen's Gold Medal for Poetry.

She published only two more novels, in 1939 *Over The Frontier* and in 1949 her own favourite, *The Holiday*: all her novels are published by Virago.

Stevie Smith died in 1971. In 1975 her *Collected Poems* were published, a selected Penguin edition appearing in 1978. The best of her brilliant short stories, essays, reviews, poems and letters are collected in *Me Again*: *The Uncollected Writings of Stevie Smith*, published by Virago in 1981.

Virago

If you would like to know more about Virago books, write to us at Ely House, 37 Dover Street, London W1X 4HS for a full catalogue.

Please send a stamped addressed envelope

VIRAGO
Advisory Group

THE HOLIDAY

*

STEVIE SMITH

WITH AN INTRODUCTION
by
JANET WATTS

Published by VIRAGO PRESS Limited 1979
Ely House, 37 Dover Street, London W1X 4HS

Reprinted 1980, 1981

Copyright © Stevie Smith 1949

First published by Chapman and Hall 1949

This edition copyright © James MacGibbon 1971

Introduction Copyright © Janet Watts, 1979, 1981

Printed in Great Britain by litho at
The Anchor Press, Tiptree, Essex

British Library Cataloguing in Publication Data
Smith, Stevie
    The holiday, or, Work it out for yourself
    I. Title
    823'. 912 (F)   PR6037. M43
    ISBN 0-86068-067-3

INTRODUCTION

Stevie Smith was first and last a poet, not a novelist. She didn't much like writing prose, and produced her first novel purely to get into print. The publisher to whom she submitted some poems in 1935 told her to 'go away and write a novel', and she went back to him in a matter of weeks with *Novel On Yellow Paper*: but this book, which brought her a sudden celebrity on its publication by Jonathan Cape in 1936, did not please her greatly. Many years later she told Kay Dick that there was a lot in it she disliked – 'partly the manner. I don't quite know where that manner comes from' (*Ivy and Stevie*, 1971).

She much preferred *The Holiday*, her third novel; pronouncing it (again to Kay Dick) '*beautiful*: never brassy like *Novel On Yellow Paper*, but so richly melancholy like those hot summer days when it is so full of that calm before the autumn, it quite ravishes me. When I read it, the tears stream down my face because of what Matthew Arnold says, you know:

> "But oh, the labour,
> O Prince, what pain".'

Not everyone was of the same opinion. It took Stevie Smith some years to find a publisher for this novel, which she wrote and set in the England of the Second World War. When it was finally published in 1949, she was obliged to alter all its references to the current war to a more topical phenomenon she called 'the post-war'; and the book's original typescript shows how, by a few changes in the wording, she gave political discussions like the ones on India a new validity for 1949.

For some readers *The Holiday* is even more idiosyncratic than its two prose companions. 'A terribly difficult book to read,' in the view of Stevie Smith's last publisher; 'a lot of it, Stevie, is really poems, you know.' Certainly we find in this novel the same unique sensibility that informs her poetry: the sensibility that perceived the dreadful comicality of pain, and expressed it in what is her most famous and unforgettable image: the swimmer far out at sea, whose jolly-looking wave is really the flailing despair of a drowning man.

> *Not Waving but Drowning*
>
> Nobody heard him, the dead man,
> But still he lay moaning:
> I was much further out than you thought
> And not waving but drowning.
>
> Poor chap, he always loved larking
> And now he's dead
> It must have been too cold for him his heart gave way,
> They said.
>
> Oh, no no no, it was too cold always
> (Still the dead one lay moaning)
> I was much too far out all my life
> And not waving but drowning.

It is a sensibility that was for all its isolation dynamically at one with the spirit of her time.

Stevie Smith is at the centre of this novel, as of all her works. She was Pompey in *Novel On Yellow Paper*: she is Celia in *The Holiday*. Celia has an office life at 'the Ministry' and a home life shared with an old aunt in a London suburb; Stevie Smith worked for years in a publisher's office in central London and lived with her old aunt in a house in Palmers Green that was her home from the age of three until her death at sixty-eight in 1971.

In *The Holiday* Celia leaves her Ministry and her home and takes a train to the north to stay with her clerical uncle Heber. She is accompanied by Casmilus, an adored cousin, and Tiny, a likeable colleague dogged by a brother whom everyone detests. They walk and ride and eat summer meals; wrangle, bicker, giggle; love and hate each other in waves of affection and frustration; talk and fall silent.

Celia is whimsical, fragile; she cries often (though her tears are many times deleted from the original typescript). In her anguish at the painfulness of living, she – like her creator – courts and craves for death. (One friend warned Stevie Smith crisply that she would probably not find him half the dish she imagined.) Yet Celia, like Stevie, is also dry and wry: irritated by the mournful Tiny, unmoved by his masochistic love. The melancholy of *The Holiday*, in which Stevie Smith took such retrospective pleasure, is leavened by wit; its prevailing unhappiness – 'Why are we so sad: is it the war, is it the post-war?' – transformed by humour and jokes.

Celia declares that she hates opinions – 'the worst sort of conversation' – yet the novel is patchworked with them. Here is chat about the middle classes and the public schools; conversation about the war and post-war; discussion of Africa, India, America, Africa. And stories. Stories that are Celia's delight and her defence, against both her own and her friends' unhappiness. Stories of cats and apes and eagles to distract and entertain; family stories that she knows backwards and loves to hear again over a leisurely breakfast or in the middle of a wakeful night. Stories from religion and history; stories (like 'Over-dew') she has written and failed to get published; stories of old secrets, fragrant with the dust of concealment.

There is a love story in *The Holiday*, too. Celia loves Casmilus, 'my beloved wise cousin, my solemn friend. Why do I fret and cry because he can be nothing else than a friend?' But cry she does. The novel is full of the pain of love. 'Yes, everybody is hankering after it and whining,' says Celia, to comfort the woebegone Tiny. 'This hunger we have is a good thing, it is the long shin bone that shows the child will grow tall.' (For all her own pain, she is a great cheerer-upper.)

Stevie Smith never married, and always insisted that her own best element was friendship, not love.

> My spirit in confusion,
> Long years I strove,
> But now I know that never
> Nearer I shall move,
> Than a friend's friend to friendship,
> To love than a friend's love.

One important friendship was with George Orwell, whose portrait has been recognised in the character of Basil in *The Holiday*. Literary gossip has linked their names in a love affair: but a mutual woman friend of them both insists that although 'George was definitely one of Stevie's chum's, there was always a distance in Stevie's chummy relationships, and she 'would have felt nervous if it got too sexual'. Yet her feelings were intense, even fierce. The year before her death she told a friend

viii

that he must correct people's mis-conception of her, that 'because I never married I know nothing about the emotions. When I am dead you must put them right. I loved my aunt.'

The love in *The Holiday* is a strangled love; even the affection is restrained. The book is suffused with an overcast luminance, a subdued warmth. Celia rides close to her cousin on the old horse Noble. 'We are silent . . . and I feel very strongly the friendship of my sad cousin, that is not usually sad but laughing, and the friendship of Tiny, and the friendship of the sweet mute Heber, and I wish it might always be so . . .'

Yet this tranquillity is not the lasting tone of this book, as it was not of its author. 'I was always a troubled person,' Stevie Smith once said. 'I have never changed.' From her friends we have accounts of the drastic extremes of her moods: one of them has described a typical lunch passed in 'fits of laughter', followed by agonised moments when Stevie dissolved in tears in the Ladies' and spoke of suicide: only to waltz out again with renewed gaiety to try on silly hats in Fenwicks all afternoon.

So with Celia. The cosiness of wartime (or post-war) England does not warm her desolation. For her the cheerful routine of the office stops as short of real solace as a merry-go-round jerked abruptly to a halt. 'When one pauses for a moment . . . what does it all add up to, and what is this work that is so bustling and so cosy?' She runs from the amusingness of parties – which she expertly evokes – to rest her head against a marble doorpost. 'This sadness cuts down again upon me, it is like death. The bright appearance of the friends at the parties makes it a terrible cut, like a deep sharp knife, that has cut deep, but not quite yet away.'

We relish Stevie Smith's wit; we bask in her moments of quietness and calm. But we cannot forget her pain. At the end of 'the best, the longest' day of her holiday, she sits by the seaside with her loved cousin, and cries and screams: 'such a pain in my heart' makes her teacup fall from her hand, and 'twisted my heart and muscles, so that I was bent backwards as though it was an overdose of strychnine'.

The sound of that scream echoes through this gentle book. Something in *The Holiday*'s original typescript gives it an even deeper resonance, and provides a still more poignant glimpse into the strange, lonely spirit of this gifted writer.

Celia awakes from a bad dream, 'so tired, and so sad'. What was it about?

> There is the sea, and one wishes to get into it, but there are always so many things to do, and the end of the holiday comes, and still there is the sea, and still one has not got into it, one has forgotten to get into the sea, but that is what one has most wished to do, so strongly one has wished to do that, and now the holiday is over. So in my sleep I must have cried and struggled, for there are tears on my cheek, and I am quite exhausted. . . '

The passage is excised with a vigorous hand. The sort of hand that waves cheerfully from far out at sea? In the paradoxical world of Stevie Smith, a poet might drown, even without getting her feet wet.

Janet Watts, 1978

x

I

I WAS working over some figures with Tiny at the Ministry; it was a figure code. Tiny sighed and hummed under his breath.

Oh, Tiny, don't hum.

Well, all right. Or I can go into the next room. Or you can.

We can't very well do that. I leaned over Tiny and whispered in his ear. We can't very well do that because Clem is there.

Oh Lord, I keep forgetting. Oh how I wish they hadn't moved him into Section V. Oh dear, oh dear.

Well as long as we *remember*, we can think of something else. These cablegrams, for instance. I sighed. What do you make of number seven?

Yes, said Tiny, there's something about figures.

Something like work, I said. Only don't hum, Tiny, that spoils it, that we can do without.

I think our colleagues Eleanor and Constance are awfully nice women, said Tiny with such a generous beaming look.

Why, Tiny, you do look happy. It is the figures that make you feel that way about Eleanor and Constance. They always seem so occupied, those two, especially Eleanor seems so occupied.

We were born under a no-grip star, said Tiny.

Yes, that's it, I said, we are lucky to be in this room

together, that is something one might not have looked for.

When I see old Eleanor crashing about with that con-
centrated look on her face, you would think the whole of
the post-war hung up on her. It is like the Saki lady who
was in touch with all the Governments of Europe before
breakfast. . . .

Now, Tiny, I said, that is not quite in the mood.

What do *you* make of Number Seven? said Tiny.

I took it over to the window and began singing 'From
Greenland's Icy Mountains' to myself.

You've got the words mixed up, said Tiny crossly, I don't
see that that is very much better than my humming.

I sang the verse again more loudly:

> From Greenland's icy mountains
> From India's coral strand
> Where Afric's golden fountains
> Roll down the something land
> From many a lonely hamlet
> Which hid by beech and pine
> Like an eagle's nest hangs on the crest
> Of purple Apennine.

You see, said Tiny, it doesn't even fit in very well. You
have to joggle that last line but one a bit.

At this moment the door opened and my cousin Casmilus
came into the room.

Hallo, Tiny. I say, Celia, I want to speak to you.

Oh all right, said Tiny, I'm going.

Just as he was starting off Clem put his head round the
door.

I want you, Tiny, he said. Just popping round to the
A.B.C., eh? Well, if you could spare me a few minutes first.

The two brothers went out together.

How crestfallen our poor Tiny looks, said Caz when they had gone.

Clem is a really horrible person, I said.

Tiny isn't much better.

I find Tiny very *sympathisch* on the contrary.

Caz flicked the cigarette ash off his battle-dress trousers and came and stood over me. He said he was passing through London on his way to the north.

Oh, what is it Caz, what is it you want to say? Oh Caz, I said, I am so cold.

We went and stood on the hearthrug by the empty fire-place. Caz put his head on my shoulder. It is cold outside to-day. I often feel quite at a loss, he said, and rubbed his nose close into my neck.

Some days, I said, are long and thin and there is nothing in them, and the peace goes badly, it goes very badly for us, and to-day there is a note to say that America ... that Russia ... England, I said, is stretched out and thin. I feel....

What do you feel? I suppose one does not kill oneself for Russia ... for America. And so on. What do you feel?

I feel that I am frozen. It is cold *inside* too.

Caz rocked me gently backwards and forwards. I often feel quite lost, he said, quite lost.

Caz, I said, when I am with people, I do not feel so cold. I like to sit in the tube train to watch the people and be watched. The light and the warmth of the train brings the faces to life. They are alive alive-o, that before was wandering in a desert of night dreams with landscapes. Here on the underground train, I said (as we rocked more violently and the cold rainstorm beat from outside upon the window pane, rat-tat, rat-tat, as if it were hailstones, but it is a June shower) in the tube train, I said it is very different. We have left

7

behind us the dreams and the scenery; we are together, we are good humoured, we have good manners we have the excellent unconscious good manners of off-hand civil London. We do not talk to each other—my word that could be a burden—but we smile, or perhaps a person may say something about the weather; that is nothing more than a smile. But first I said (hurrying a little) we must come on the escalator where there is the Notice the sharp Dean put in his journalism for a moral lesson, 'Stand on the Right and Let the Others Pass You'. I sighed. During the war, I said, it was getting late, and when we went down to the platform the mother was putting the baby to bed, it is on the top shelf of the bunk-stand he sleeps, so she is tucking him in, she says: 'You lay there, oh what wicked eyes you've got.' And in the train there is now some rush and confusion as the American soldiers come in. The man who is sitting next to my sister beckons me across to change seats with him so that I can sit beside her. A woman gets in with a rolled mattress and seven children. The American soldier who is standing kissing his girl does not move; he is in a desert with his girl. . . .

Everybody feels that he is cold and lost, said Caz, but not everybody will say as much, a lot of people will say that it is very jolly and will bite the people who say it is not; it is better that people should know that they are cold and lost.

And he went on to say that there was a lot of the war left over from the fighting times, I do not know, he said, that we can bear not to be at war.

I agree; always there is some more war to be written about. Just now, I said, I am having to write a paper about De Gaulle, and the beginnings of his movement, and the beginnings of the Resistance, and of his Rassemblement du Peuple Français. It seems we had to pull De Gaulle out of

France and build up the resistance movement. Eh, well, did we not have to do this? Caz, I said, I am very pro-English. England has the seas, the islands, the continents and the straits, at each point she is vulnerable. She must fight and build up her credits, and fight upon a hundred fronts. I think De Gaulle is the most awfully silly chap. Why are the English surprised that they are now hard up, well it is rather surprising that they are surprised, it would be surprising I should say if the English were not very poor indeed by this time.

Caz said: If the French could form a government that would last one week, that would be something. Can a country be civilized that cannot form a government?

Sentimental persons, I said, prefer always the revolutionary times, with the king over the water and a free wind blowing. . . . sed victa Catoni, ahem, that is where they feel at home. And so forth. But I like better the time that is more crucial than revolution, that is the time when revolution succeeds and must govern. And I thought: Can resistance pass to government and not take to itself the violence of its oppressors, the absolutism and the torture? Will it do so in Palestine, in India? It is our nature, I said, to fret and feel cold and lost. Mark my words, Caz, crisis and exile are our lot. The English are right not to make a plan, they know that the stream cannot rise higher than its source, they will not make an absolute plan, to form man as a manufactury, they will not be so foolish and so wicked as to do this; and yet they govern, they feel their way along.

Caz said that he was very pro-English, too, but that they were damned irritating, too, with the appearance of being a shade disingenuous, since they obviously could not be so stupid as they seemed, and must therefore be accounted sly.

Oh well, I said, I suppose it doesn't do us any harm to be poor now for a bit.

Caz went on to say that the Germans in their careful way had always made a great study of the English and might almost be said to graduate in it. But sure enough, though they might say the 'English race' was biological, and how the English sat in front of their damned smoky fires, just staring into them and not doing a thing about the draught under the door—'just loungin' and sufferin' like you Celia, just loungin' and sufferin'' all the same sooner or later they were bound to trip up, as with the fake prisoner-of-war letters they shot down over England with the bombs, so that No. 44 Acacia Grove, Bermondsey, might be laid flat, but floating down upon the owner, maybe fathom-deep in rubble, would be this fake letter from Harry-boy to say how fine the Germans were being to him in his sta-lag, and what decent chaps they were, and how much they loved the English, et cetera. Only of course they couldn't know, they got it wrong, the poor Germans couldn't know—for all they read his letters—that boy Harry never said 'darling' to his Mum, and had never so much as mentioned the Germans, one way or the other, not during the whole long years he was in camp; and how he always said in every letter 'least said soonest mended'. So all the way from 'Dear Mum and Dad' to 'all the best, Harry', there was nothing in Harry's letters the most college-raised chap in Deutschland, not by industry nor cunning, could lay his hand to for a true-twist propaganda pill.

Maybe, Caz went on, maybe what they hoped was that the mum and dad would write back kindly-like to Harry to say that his letter had arrived safely along with the bomb-o, and that No. 44 Acacia Grove was now standing there no more, which would be a tick on the chart for them, and a headache for Harry. Oh, Celia, said Caz when we had got to the end of these recitals, I do feel lost, well that is what you are always saying isn't it? I d-o-o fee-eel l-o-ost.

He stepped away from me for a few steps and began to look rather vacant.

What's the matter, Caz?

Oh, nothing. I say, are you going to Lopez's party to-night?

Ye-es I a-a-am.

You are very flip at the parties I suppose?

Yes I am.

It is not much good, is it? said Caz. 'Something human,' he said, 'is dearer to me than the wealth of all the world.'

Oh, yes, that is how it is.

But you remember, Celia, who said that, he was not human at all.

He lived in the black mountains, I said.

No need to cry about it, dear girl.

In the black mountains, sang Caz, mimicking and getting rather louder.

> In the black mountains, feeling rather lost,
> In the black mountains and the bitter frost.

A great pounding now came on the wall.

Hush, I said, it's Clem.

Starp pounding, yelled Caz, in an affected accent.

I say, said Clem, opening the door, do shut up you two.

So long, Clem, said Caz, I'm off.

He now turned to me again and reminded me that my leave was due in a fortnight's time and asked me to come to Uncle Heber's with him. It will make a nice change for you, he said, a nice change. Will you?

Yes, I will.

Then that's settled. So long, Celia.

So long, Caz, let me hear from you.

Tiny came back into the room. He was holding a telegram in his hand.

Oh Tiny; not another telegram.

Yes it is, he said, it's the Research one, that old press cable you were looking for about De Gaulle. He began to read it out aloud, in a slow important rather breathless voice, for a practice piece, not to stammer, for Tiny suffered from a stammer.

To criticisms mainly emanating examerica that freefrench movement was largely military movement only dash this occurring proobvious reasons first sudden collapse france second men bordeaux vichy stopped departures exfrance third general lassitude to put it politeliest proseveral years of majority french politicians undash degaulle said he anxiousest more responsible french politicians should be associated cumhim but sharpliest protested antisuggestion camille chautemps would be suitable colleague quote eye appreciate joke as well as anyone but twas chautemps who signed capitulation bordeaux abandoned allies disarmed or neutralised french colonial empire and sentenced leaders freefrench deathwards unquote stop general degaulle postremarking he unthought hed see andre christophe again.

Tiny sighed, he looked quite pale. Eye appreciate joke, I do not.

II

IT IS a wonderfully successful party at Lopez's this
evening. It is a year or so after the war. It cannot be said that
it is war, it cannot be said that it is peace, it can be said
that it is post-war; this will probably go on for ten years.
Most of us at this party are working in Ministries in Relief,
in Relations, on Committees, on Commissions, clearing up,
sorting, settling, we are also writing and broadcasting. The
post-war works upon us, we are exasperated, we feel that
we are doing nothing, we work long hours, but what is it,
eh? so we feel guilty too. But at this party we are very
happy and we take hold of our happiness to make something
of it for the moment.

Lopez is living in a house in Glebe Place, she is the sister of
Clem and Tiny. She gives us spam, ham, tongue, liver-
sausage, salad-cream, cherries, strawberries (out of tins),
whisky and beer. But there is a love-feeling in the room that is
more than the beer and the whisky. Yes, there is this quick
love-feeling and much pleasure that is more than whisky.

Our friend Raji is at this party, he is the most intelligent
Indian in London. Raji has this fine intelligence and a warm
heart. He is an honest person upon a centre fixed. This is
rare, and rare indeed in an Indian. He has been in an English
prison-camp in India and has been beaten up by the Indian
police. He says that the Indians are abysmally childish.

Raji makes us laugh. He says he was with an English

13

friend and two Indians in a restaurant. The Indians said: 'Oh yes, we do not mind white people, of course, but every now and then there is beginning to run this feeling that we do not so much like them. Oh yes, now we are beginning to have to combat this disgusting and so un-free colour sense, but for the fastidious Indian there is for instance the smell of the white person. Yes, heigh-ho, that is how we are now getting.'

So we laugh too. It is wonderful that Raji can be so generous and so free, for his upbringing was in an oppressed atmosphere.

The talk is now political-historical, but presently the pace quickens, for a girl says that when she was at school. . . .

Oh yes, the pace quickens for all of us, for this is from the horse's mouth. The other talk, the history, the politics talk, is fine, too, but so often it falls down, because we are doing nothing, and so we wring our hands, the talk falls down, we are *activistes manqués*, it is Edwin and Morcar the Earls of the North. It is all that, it is a desert.

So this girl says that at school the English mistress was pestered by the Science mistress, and to avoid her must sleep in the head-mistress's bedroom. And Lopez said that at her Convent School if two girls walked alone the nun would call through the megaphone to hurry up and find a third, for never might two girls walk alone together. So this gave a chance to the lonely ones, for these lonely girls, by being good covermen, might grow chums.

No now the conversation is running on a good scent. Lopez tells us that her cousin Mary was at a Convent School and she also dearly loved the nun who taught her English literature. Mary said she was a skinny little thing with blue eyes.

This nun never knew of Mary's dear love, though for

14

years Mary wrote to her, but she kept her letters only friendly, as an old-fashioned honourable man will do for years to come, when he has an attachment for a married woman he will do this. But when Mary was in Paris on her honeymoon, she left her husband and went off to the Convent to the dear one.

The conversation now turned again to politics, for Tengal the brilliant scientist and C.P. Member came in with the poet Blind; and with them also came Clem with a heavy swagger, and behind him Tiny looking nervous and unhappy.

Tengal said that if people did not get the Workers' Front very soon, they would be walking down the street asking for it.

Every political movement, said Tiny, in a low and stammering voice, ha-ha-has its m-m-middle period, has it not, do you think? And w-w-what do you suppose the Party Chiefs are doing?

This was perhaps too bold a flutter.

Why yes, said Clem, has anybody thought of that?

The Workers' Front, I said, there is a horrible cant sound about that, it runs with the crypto-fascist and the Red Dog, and the fascist beast, it is something that makes people laugh, it makes nonsense of it. . . .

It is not the moment for the clean sweep, said Tiny.

Or perhaps it is the moment, said Tengal, and it is the moment and it is already gone.

Tiny sank down beside me on the sofa and buried his face in his hands.

There was now a loud crash from outside and Captain Maulay came bounding into the room with a paper bag full of cream buns.

That was Violet's bathroom window, he said, she's

always trying to make the water run hot and now the geyser's blown up.

He handed a cream bun to Lopez and went to get a drink.

Tengal said if it had not been for England, there would by this time have been a united states of Europe.

United in *what?* said Tiny.

I now go and sit in the corner to have some conversation with Basil Tait.

Is Caz in London?

No, he has gone to the North.

I am furious with Basil this evening because Basil is collecting some drawings for a book of drawings that are to be representative of this and that. So he has kept my drawings for a long time to choose from them, but he does not get on with this, so I say: If you cannot choose the drawings why do you not give them to Raji to choose?

Basil said that it was mischievous of Clem to speak in the House of Lords as he did about the Jewish National State.

I hate the petty nationalismus idea, I said, this idea will be the death of the Peace, when the post-war is over and the Peace comes, you will see it will be the death of it. Nothing that Clem says at any time or in any place is for any one thing but the advantage of Clem.

There is nobody who speaks about the Jewish National State, said Basil, who has not some other idea at heart.

So Basil also hates the petty nationalismus idea, so for a moment there is a little piece of rapprochement between us.

I say, since it does not matter at all what you put in your old book, why do you not put my drawings in it?

Basil says: Do you think that paper the *Smallholder* would

16

have advertisements in it for wire netting to put in front of my Angora rabbit hutch?

And I smile at Basil and I say: Tired of all these, for restful death I cry, as to behold desert a beggar born.

Basil says, I like people to have a good opinion of their work.

Tiny slips by on his way out. So long, Celia, he says, I'll pop into the Ministry on my way back, no need to bother Clem.

What an ass he is, said Basil.

He is not an ass, I say, he has a very suffering time, he is this suffering persecuted creature, if he had not been at Eton with you, but had grown up a ground dog in low conditions, he would have all your strength to help and your sympathy to warm.

A young Indian friend of Raji's now comes across the room and sits down beside us. He is called Behar.

I hope I am not interrupting a sentimental interlude, he says.

Oh yes, says Basil, the conversation is very sentimental in this corner.

Yes, *rather*, I say, it is just like that, but please do not mind, Behar dear.

Behar tells us what he was saying to Sir Stafford Cripps, 'Stafford, you are an abject character'.

Go on, Behar, you didn't.

Oh yes, I did, said Behar, I meant it too.

That's right, Behar dear. Isn't Behar wonderful, Basil? What did Cripps say?

Oh nothing.

I expect he blushed, didn't he, tell us how he blushed, Behar.

Behar got rather huffy. Behar said he was at a party and there were some most grand important people there, like it was the meeting of the Inner Cabinet with Lord Cherwell under the table. There was an Indian friend of Behar's there. Behar tells us how this one was very short with the English.

Oh, he said, I never knew anyone so blunt with the English before, very short he was.

And how did the English grand people take it, Behar, how did they take this shortness of your friend?

Lying down, said Behar.

Lying down?

Yes, lying down.

And snoring?

Yes, snoring, no, no.

Not snoring?

No of course, not snoring.

Captain Maulay now came across the room with what was left of the cream buns, and the conversation turned to witchcraft.

Captain Maulay said, Aleister Crowley gets results.

What sort of results? said Basil. Can he turn a two-shilling piece into half a crown, or does he get himself kicked downstairs? And he began to look around the room in rather a bored way.

What are you looking for, Basil? I said.

I thought your cousin Tom might be here.

Oh no, Tom never goes to parties.

Neither of your cousins is here, said Basil with a smile.

Captain Maulay began to talk about a lady Pythoness he frequents in the King's Road. She is called Madame Sopa.

She has a real gift said Maulay, she has sometimes been called in by Scotland Yard.

Called *in?* said Basil.

Yes they are not always certain whether it is murder or suicide.

Oh.

Once, he said, there was a murder—I always think of it in that way—committed in my drawing room. It was when I was living at 259 Sloane Street. He sighed. My wife had invited some very well known people, it was an extremely well-attended party. The Maharajah of Trincha was there. He sighed again. That was before my poor wife died.

But the murder? I said.

Well, said Maulay, a member of the band, he was the cornet sitting next to the drums, was suddenly found stabbed. They brought it in as suicide. But mark my words, Miss Phoze, not for nothing was a representative of Scotland Yard at the inquest. No, it was murder. But the India Office wanted the matter hushed up, because they wanted to get the Maharajah back to India so that they could depose him. He was a rotten fellow, a thoroughly bad hat. He once had a horse of his thrashed to death.

Good heavens, said Basil, not in England surely?

Oh no, it was in India.

And what did Madame Sopa say?

Madame Sopa? Oh, yes. Well, she knew nothing about it at the time, you know, but a few months later I was taking her over the house. . . .

At 259 Sloane Street?

Yes. And when we went into the drawing room where the murder—or suicide as they said—was committed, Madame Sopa clutched my arm. Get me out of here quick, she said, and then she screamed. She said that something was trying to get hold of her. When I told her what had happened in that room, she said it was the spirit of the dead man trying to tell her it was murder and not suicide.

Maulay turned to me. What do you make of that, eh?

Basil said he thought it was pretty thick of the India Office to hush it up.

Oh, I don't know, said Maulay, after all the poor chap was dead wasn't he?

What are you doing for your leave-holiday this year? Basil asked me.

I am going to Uncle Heber's.

Will Tom be there?

No, Tom never goes to his father's. You know that Tom will never see his father.

Oh yes, of course. And Caz?

Oh yes, Caz will be there.

That must make it rather worse for Heber, said Basil, still smiling. Yes, the nephew will come, but not the son.

It was Caz who suggested that I should come to Heber's with him.

Oh, Heber, is always glad to see *you*, and so is Caz, of course.

Maulay now handed me a betting slip.

Look at that, he said, fourteen guineas on the wrong side. He sighed. She's no good with horses, that's a fact. I said to her, Sopa, why on earth didn't you stick to your first choice, we should have made a packet between us. But no, she said she liked the look of the jockey. And that's the result.

Basil said you never could tell with a gift like that.

I left Basil to Maulay and ran out of the room and put my head against the cold marble of the door post. Tengal came running after me with a furious look.

Celia, he said, you must stop this, what is the matter?

It is the conversation, said Raji, who had followed us on his way to the kitchen to fetch something for Lopez. Basil is not in a good mood this evening and Maulay is always a terrible trying chap.

Raji's happy black face looked down smiling at me. He said, I really only came this evening because I thought your cousin would be here.

My cousin Caz?

Yes, Caz of course.

Not Tom?

Oh—*Tom*.

III

AFTER THE party is over Lopez and I get some cocoa and carry it up to our bedrooms. Lopez's bedroom is very untidy, there is the house-agreement from Monet Mogram, and the letters, and the B.B.C. contracts, and the first typings of manuscripts. We talk till four o'clock, then I go to my room, but I cannot sleep. At six o'clock I get up and have another look at the venetian blind and now I see how to pull it up, so I pull it up and open the sash window wide and look at the catholic byzantine church that is opposite my window. The sun is shining through the grey clouds, as it is always doing this terrible summer, the effect is that London looks like a steel engraving. I get back into bed and think about writing. Lopez has this method, she has a quick ear and a wonderful gift for mimicry. She will for instance overhear a remark in the street. It is rather like the competition for the best overheard remark, like the woman at the all-in wrestling match who said, Proper ape, ain't he? or the Chekhov play remark, Makes you worry doesn't it? or the bus remark, A little further along, dearie, I never could abide a warm seat, it's the aura, I think. And for a competition it is all right. But in writing, though it is very good in Lopez's writing, it is not always so good, because it is so often something that gets an effect of significance, that is without significance. It is often indeed being an offence against the people, because it is without understanding. So it does not, oh it does not show what people are like. But what the hell does that matter, for when you get George Moore, with his woman painter and her wife in *Celibate Lives*, or his Esther, or Arnold Bennett with his *Elsie and the Child*, what do you do but throw up your hands and say: These are people and what the hell can you do with them? It is like the countess in Maurice Baring's book who said to the young man: You write books, yes? So what are they about? Oh, people, said the young man. People? said the countess—ah, they are very difficult.

I lie in bed thinking about Lopez's writing, and Raji's writing and my writing, and how exasperating and difficult it all is. And I think of that noble character, my Uncle Heber, with whom I shall soon be staying to have my leave holiday (oh how I wish it was now the time to go down to my Uncle Heber's and that I should not have first to wait for a fortnight to go by), so I think what he said, it was when a large party of distracting people had come to tea at the rectory, and at last had gone home again. He said: 'Solitude, reform and silence.'

At nine o'clock Lopez brings some bread and cheese and coffee on a tray for breakfast, but no butter; and we have some more talk, and I go home.

Going home in Brompton Road outside Harrods I met my cousin Tom Fox. This Tom is Heber's son, but he makes a desolation of the relationship, he makes a desolation for himself, and in Lincolnshire Heber weeps for his son.

It is too early for a drink so we go into Harrods and have some coffee and some lemon curd tarts.

Tom was once mad for six months, and for this six months

23

he was shut away in a fine mansion in Clapton where they have cures for these nervous disorders.

This house belonged to the De Vere family, but now it is surrounded by the Clapton shops and flats, by the busy streets and the busy practical people. It is a little eccentric now that was once set out in dignity in the empty marshlands close by the river.

Tom recovered from his madness; he was a brave patient who wished only to find again his Tom-identity; he worked with the doctors and grew better. But many people in that house did not grow better, and later they went somewhere else. It was curious that it should be this De Vere mansion, because always Tom had the Shakespeare-Bacon-De Vere sonnet-bug biting at him, and in his madness the laughter would run from him as he made the brilliant cypher puns.

I went to see him when he was mad. He had a long low room giving through french windows on to a quiet garden. It is fine to lie here, he said, and watch the sunshine in the garden, and watch the nurses go to and fro, but I wish the nurse would not turn into a black cat, it is distracting to see that. And then again he used to laugh, choking and snoring a little in his throat.

Since Tom has come out from the De Vere mansion his manner to me is warmer and closer, that before was only friendly. He will come into my room at the Ministry, and suddenly he will be there, and he will say 'Celia'.

Tom's treatment of his father is atrocious. My cousin Caz thinks that Tom is an abject character, a weak cruel creature, no good at all. Look what he has done to Heber, he says, look what this precious cousin of ours has done to that patient saint in Lincolnshire, who sits and weeps for his son. There is your Tom for you.

But I have a warm feeling of friendship and pity for Tom

24

and have never been afraid of him. But always one feels that he may become mad again—'Celia'.

He will come loping into my room with his long mad stride, and he will fetch up against a piece of furniture, stooping his long body against it, and he will look out of his blue eyes with a mad look, and he will say 'Celia'.

This has got on Tiny's nerves and always Tiny says: Well, so long, Celia, I'll run out now for a bit. And off he goes round the blocks to the A.B.C.

Tom will look at me; say no more than 'Celia'; and go.

What a pity that I do not love Tom as I love Caz. What a pity that Caz is not in the simple *cousinly* relationship of mad Tom; ah it is a pity, that old scandal-story that makes Caz nearer in blood than a cousin, it is a pity.

But there is something anarchic in my poor Tom that presses. One grows sad, the times run sadly, the person feels lost, the person grows desperate, the person is already half-way mad.

So Tom's madness stretched out and met in me something that was also mad, or rather—willing to be mad. Yes, in the person who is sane but who is willing to be mad it is the will that has broken.

Tom has been for three years a professor of English at Tokio University.

One day Tom came into my room and said something more than 'Celia'; he said: You must promise to do this, put your hand here and promise.

He asked me to have dinner with him and afterwards to go back with him to the studio where he makes his broadcast talk for the China Station.

How can a mad person do such a thing as to make a learned talk for the China Station? Tom was not mad in such a way that he could not make the most learned discourse for Eastern savants.

The person who is sane but is willing to be mad at once begins to tell himself a lot of lies, a thing that no mad person will take the trouble or indeed have the wits to think necessary to do. So I began to tell myself that my dear Tom now needed something that I could give him, the close company and the ready ear; and that as I was myself at this time lost and sad, this evening company with Tom would make for me also a little light and warmth, that there would be good will on both sides, a remembered loving friendship of long standing; et cetera. I also told myself that, as a matter of plain sense, it was necessary to get Tom out of the Ministry as soon as possible, and that the best way to do this was to say: Yes, yes I will come.

So now in the tea shop at Harrods he begins again about the dinner party, and I say: Yes, yes, I will. And Tom says: Give me your hand, promise. And I give him my hand and promise.

So on the promise we part, and I come home to my suburb.

When I get home, it is Saturday morning. My Aunt and I have a long talk, sitting in the room at the back of the house, and I tell my Aunt that I am going to Uncle Heber's for my holiday, so then my Aunt begins to tell me the stories about my Uncle Heber when he was a little boy, and later, grown older but before he went into the church, how Heber had a little sailing boat called the *Nyad* and in this he used to go sailing on the River Humber, and his sister, that in my dear Aunt, used to go sailing with him, though the smell of the oily beastly stove made her sick, but still she would go, and how the *Nyad* was often aground on the Humber mud banks, so that Heber and my Aunt must wade ashore. paddling through the thick mud, and a sight to be seen, when at length they arrived on firm land.

So, with the smell of the lovely Humber mud in my nose, for I remember the river when I stayed at Ferraby as a young child, and never was there such a river as the Humber at Ferraby for wide vistas and mud and the water moving with dignity, and the far bank a mile away and the general and noble feeling that the world is newly come, and that there is nothing alive at this early time but only the Early Lizard, and that he is at this moment asleep in his mud, as I wrote in my poem: 'In that high and early time, There was no good deed and no crime, No oppression by informèd Mind, no knowledge and no Human Kind.'

So with these happy thoughts in my mind, I go down to our butcher, with whom my Aunt has dealt for forty years, and Mr. Montgomery the butcher gives me six ounces more than the ration book says. He is a tall thin man, looking like Charles II, he smiles as he wraps the parcel. There you are, my dear. How's Mother? (for he is convinced that my Aunt is my mother).

My mother died when I was a child, my Aunt has always lived with us, she has never wished to marry, she has 'no patience' with men (she also had 'no patience' with Hitler). She thinks men are soppy, she says: He is a very soppy man, a most soppy individual.

I love my Aunt, I love her, I love the life in the family, my familiar life, but I like also to go out and to see how the other people get along, and especially I like to see how the married ladies get along, and I sit and listen and watch, and I see how much they think about their husbands, even if they hate 'em like hell there is this thought, this attention.

27

How can you keep it up, Maria? I ask the women friends, I think you are absolutely marvellous to keep on thinking about them and listening to them and having the children and keeping the house going on turning round the men. I have never had such a thing heigh-ho.

And they are at first immensely pleased about this that I have been saying, but then they begin to wish not to stress how martyr-like wonderful it is, and they begin to say how much one is missing if one does not have it; so I have had trouble with my married women friends, and with those who are living free-like and unmarried with their darling chosen one, I have had trouble for two reasons, because sometimes I like the chosen-one too much, but mostly and the most trouble, because I do not like him enough, and because I think it is so wonderful of the women to be so unselfish and so kind. But I can see that they have to do it, if they are going to have a darling husband and a darling home of their own and darling children, they have to do it, there is no other way, and if you do not then you will live lonely and grow up to old solitude. Amen.

But most women, especially in the lower and lower-middle classes, are conditioned early to having 'father' the centre of the home-life, with father's chair, and father's dinner, and father's *Times* and father says, so they are not brought up like me to be this wicked selfish creature, to have no boring old father-talk, to have no papa at all that one attends to, to have a darling Aunt to come home to, that one admires, that is strong, happy, simple, shrewd, staunch, loving, upright and bossy, to have a darling sister that is working away from home, and to be for my Aunt, with this sister, the one.

When I was getting too much the tyrant when I was a child, too domineering and too spoilt, because of being

28

the youngest and because of being ill, when I was this over-bearing invalidish creature, this objectionable baby-boss, the worst that my gentle relatives would do to me was this, they would call me 'Miss Baby'. That cut the ground from under my imperious stamping feet, that shredded the imperial purple of my infant rage, 'That will do, Miss Baby'. Mama, Auntie, Pearl, I cried then to each of them in deepest horror, for what sort of monster was I not? Then the loving hands would lift me up, and everything was now over, and quite all right, and myself the better for it, until next time. And so on.

And what points the happiness of the home life to an almost unbearable sharp point, is the running round outside the home, this home of my Aunt, my sister and myself, and the getting by, and the social play-off, as a girl like any other girl, like any other girl brought up, that is not, when I look at these others girls, that is not, oh is not the truth.

But sometimes in the running round and the play-off there is a sudden dangerous capture made, made of oneself by a person who is outside. Ah it is dangerous, then one cannot come off lightly, then one gets scorched, then one is unhappy. Very well, then, Miss Baby, it serves you right.

But it is exciting, is it not?

So now I am caught again, caught by my cousin Tom. This Tom, this lanky melancholy murderous mad one, Heber's unhappy son, the dear son of a dearer Uncle. And what should my dear Uncle Heber and my Aunt wish more than this, that I should fall in love with this cousin, and forget the other, draw Tom's madness off, draw him back to Heber, to his father who weeps for him, that I should marry Tom and bring him home?

But it is Caz I love.

My thoughts go off to an Indian childhood, there in the cool stone house, in the garden under an upright sun, Casmilus and I are running and playing, we are running arm in arm, we are running a three-legged race, and the child Raji is watching us. Snap. Another picture. We are lying in each other's arms, we are frightened of the moonlight and the jungle that pushes up to the house, we are frightened, we are together.

But my little cousin Caz's parents, eh, how did that go? The cold and learned Uncle Edmund, the not cold enough Aunt Eva, and my own free-roving loving father, my dear papa that took me out with him to make a nice stay and get better from my illness in the warm climate the doctor said? Eh, this Eva and my father, was it true?

Oh, Caz, I said, there is no proof, it is an old scandal story, a piece of eavesdropping, of mischief, why, there is no proof at all.

There is none needed, said Caz, their silence is enough.

My Aunt will never speak of Caz, she thinks I do not see him.

I am tired and happy, but restless, this day at home. At teatime I tell my Aunt that I must hurry, as I must go to the hospital to have a blood test and to give a transfusion. I did not mean to tell her.

For at once she says: You are mad to do it. And she says what the doctor said. And it is a difficult moment, for behind my Aunt's lionish kind eyes there is exasperation and anxiety, she is anxious for her girl.

I love my Aunt, my Aunt loves me. There is this straining and anxiety in this love between dear relations, but my Aunt does not know this, for she is so one-way staunch and innocent, she does not know about the strain-idea, oh it would be soppy, that would be a soppy idea.

When the performance begins, I am nervous, I lie on the high wheel bed.

It is running beautifully, says the nurse, watching the blood-flow. At once it stops. The doctor sighs.

May I try the other arm?

Oh yes.

So at last they get a pint, which is what they want for Palestine.

I come home in the ambulance, but not quite home, or my Aunt would surely have thought I was dead—Home is the dead one, home on the bier; the dead girl.

When I came home from my last leave-holiday, I cried. I said: There is not one thing in the whole of life to make it bearable.

This sadness cuts down again upon me, it is like death. And the bright appearance of the friends at the parties, makes it a terrible cut, like a deep sharp knife, that has cut deep, but not yet quite away.

IV

So now the week-end is over.

To-day at the Ministry has been a happy day and a happy social day. I am especially appointed at the Ministry to be the special assistant of two persons, these are rather high up in the Ministry, they are much higher up than my dear Tiny's odious brother Clem, they are very high indeed they are the Planners. So these two men are called Harley and Rackstraw, and to them I am dog-like runner, attendant, assistant, but most of all I do writing for them and translations and these decoding and drafting jobs that Tiny does for me, these are the cablegrams.

There are also some other people at the Ministry for whom I do writing work, there is this review I have promised to do for Raji, that he asked me to do for him at Lopez's party, and there is some reviewing that I do for a person called Sparrow, he is Jacky Sparrow, and he is in charge of Raji's department, that is Publications for Civilian Morale.

It is a cheerful all-round bustling job, and Tiny and I, in our room together, are very happy when we are in the middle of jobs. It is only when one pauses for a moment, or when one catches sight of the friends Eleanor and Constance, with the important look on their faces, that one begins to feel a little uncertain. For what does it all add up to, and what is this work that is so bustling and so cosy?

32

What is this? compared with Libya and Russia, and compared with the men who were sailing backwards and forwards to Russia, sailing upon the deadly Murmansk route? And these men had sailed that way before; they knew what it was. Eh, what are we up to, compared with the victory they got us?

One night there came to see my Aunt and me at home a man that was a naval commander, that wore his uniform and that had on it two Polar Stars, that were mounted on silver, that is the highest of the Polar Stars, for since Nelson's day they have not cast medals in gold. And these Polar Stars were to show that this man had been to the Arctic and to the Antarctic 'upon an expedition'. And those two shining Polar Stars certainly did not mean that this man had just gone to the Arctic and to the Antarctic and then cast about for home.

Then what did you do? I asked.

Oh well just something you know, that the Admiralty wanted done, and that they thought, well I think that's how its worded, that had been done according to the expectation of what their Lordships expected to be done, or within a reasonable sort of range of it. Ah yes.

So what is what we do compared with that?

When the morning had bustled itself away, with Tiny and me wrapped up in our jobs, and with nothing more unpleasant than the sounds of sneezing and coughing and nose blowing from the next room where Clem was giving himself up to a cold that he had caught on the way home from the party, lunch time came and I went and had lunch with Jacky Sparrow. He is an old friend of ours, and we are these lunching friends. He is a Yorkshire happy dog, very bright, very kind, very good, at his job he is very good. There is much talk—I get all my news from you, Celia— much laughter, some claret that his Club has still got.

33

But in the late afternoon Tom Fox comes suddenly into my room at the Ministry. Ah, this is a dangerous moment. I cannot speak or move, say yes, or no. So he asks me to have dinner with him to-morrow.

I walked slowly from the Ministry to Star Court, where I was to meet Tom. This is a club-like place looking on to the Embankment Gardens, very snug, very comfortable. I used to come here with Raji, we used to talk and laugh and talk gossip and scandal, for a whole evening without stopping. Once a fellow club-like member, sitting solitary in the drawing-room over his solitary coffee, smiled to see the way Raji and I did not once come to a pause, this was a smile of exasperation and envy. To-night with Tom it was very different. I went into the restaurant and Tom was sitting there. I thought: Surely it will be all right, it will be this dinner party, it will be something for warmth and pleasure, it can surely be this, and the dinner and the talk, surely that can be happy, and the sadness will go away, at least for the moment it will go away. But the talk was not easy and happy as it was with Raji, and the unhappiness did not go away, it became so much the worse, forcing a silence that was not between friends and could not be allowed. I thought: We are here to destroy each other, I thought that we were looking at each other like animals behind bars. I went back with him to his room at the Ministry.

Tom said: We will go into the studio. So we went into the studio. This was a cold lofty room, with a raised stage at one end and a dome with glass windows. The windows were covered with indigo blinds left over from the black-out. It was spick and span and white with a dark blue carpet.

Tom, be careful. I said: What is that noise? (There was a sound of trampling overhead.)

Oh that is only the African Section, said Tom in a low sad voice, only the African Section.

Tom, Tom, be careful.

I thought of the Barbey D'Aurevilly story I read, of the dead girl lying in French curves on the rich floor carpet, the fat beautiful woman with the narrow sloping shoulders, and the narrow waist and the fine fat hips. And underneath the picture was written *'Elle était morte et sa mort disait tout'*.

He took my head in his hands and ran his hands down to my throat. I thought: Now it is over, now it will soon be over. I broke his hands from my throat. Speak to me, I said. He did not say one word but began to weep. I took his hands from his face and held them and began to speak hurriedly to him about the golden eagles that nest in the Old Caledonian Forest and upon the Cairngorm Mountains. There are now, I said, only twenty-four of these eagles in the whole of the British Isles. A soft bright look came into Tom's eyes as I was speaking of the eagles. Tom and I together had once found an eagle's nest and we had left the eggs untouched. Listen, Tom, I spoke in a strangled voice, getting quicker: In the Cairngorms there are now six active pairs of eagles and two doubtful pairs, I sighed, while in Clova-Lochnager the six pairs which were in these parts in 1938 have now been reduced to two active pairs and two doubtful pairs. So what do we find now? I said. What we find now is this. In the two areas of Clova-Lochnager and the Cairngorms, about one-third of the total population of adult eagles has disappeared within the last twelve years. Mark my words, Tom, I said, it is the egg collector who is responsible. But also, I said, the gamekeeper in the Eastern Highlands, he is not eager to protect the eagle. I sighed: The eagle kills grouse. It is said also that it eats young lambs.

But for all that, I said, it is the grandest bird that is left to breed with us. It is the grandest bird.

I could think of no more of the golden eagle to tell Tom, and as I stopped talking the bright soft look left his eyes and he fell again into a stare.

Speak to me, I said, say something to me. He did not say one word.

When Tom was at this fine De Vere house, his friend Bo used to call for him sometimes to take him out, and to take him into the Ritz Bar, and to take him round and about in gallant company. And as Tom seemed to enjoy his pleasures in a sensible way, Bo said: Why go back, why go back to the De Vere house, why not stay with us? But Tom said, I like it, I like the silence.

So there was this madness in the silence to-night, and I thought that the madness would now come back, and that I had done this, and that it was a great injury I had done to him, and that I could not speak, but was mad too.

The African Section was still tearing heavily backwards and forwards over our heads. They appeared to be moving heavy articles of furniture about the room to try them in different positions in an indecisive mood.

The next day I am talking to my Aunt at breakfast time. For I want to know about this sadness deficiency feeling. And I believe that some other people have it, but not my Aunt, I should say not. But I believe that other people have it; and that at least is a consolation to bolster one up. Much more that is a comfort for instance than the idea to throw oneself into the work, to think of other people, to behave as if one did not have it. Eh? But that can produce suddenly the last strain, to break and destroy, that is the feeling of strain from the appearance that is one thing, and the reality that is certainly another. So I want to get to the bottom of it.

I say: Was Mama a sad girl, Auntie, did Mama have these black-dog moods when she did not hate anybody so much as herself, and not the devil more?

Your mother, said my Aunt was not a happy little girl, not so happy as she should have been. She loved your grandmother, who died when she was eleven, your Uncle Heber was then at the University, and I kept the house and the servants for your grandfather. We had the man Twigg to push the bathchair—but no, that was later—and the old dog Prince to walk beside it, and the maid Ellen who used to say, when Twigg had had rather too much to drink, the day his Army pension came—'Twigg's got 'em again'. The drink used to make him so sulky.

And for a time your Great Aunt Boyle was with us, and she said to me: 'You should persuade your father to marry again, he is a young man, you should do this.' But I said: If he wishes to marry again, he will do so, it is nobody else's business. So she went. She was a pious chapelgoing woman, and no good one to have in the house. Your grandfather could not abide nonconformists. He did not marry again, for he worshipped your grandmother. But he was a moody sad man after her death, she was so wise, and with a sure touch could draw the right people around her, and keep the sad moods away from him. She was a good wife to him, she was what a woman should be.

There was something of the Begum about my Aunt as she said this, and as she sat, presiding at the well-found breakfast table, drawing another cup of tea and helping me to the buttered haddocks; there was something of the Begum in her eagle managing eye and in the pronouncement '—what a woman should be'. Ha, ha, I thought to myself, but there was no He-Begum in your life, no there was not, Alec Ormstrode loved you, but you would have none of him, no, you were not for him 'what a woman should be'. No, you are the Begum Female Spider who has devoured her suitors and who lives on and makes these crocodile-like pronouncements, and who is like a lion with a spanking tail who will have no nonsense.

My mother, went on my Aunt, was a good wife to your Grandfather, but later, after her death, he said: 'I have no strong feeling of confidence in myself.' Although he was a very clever engineer, and had an influential position in the engineering circles, and was indeed chosen out of all the Kingdom to be Honorary Chief Engineer to the Royal Naval Reserve—there were only two of them and he was one—he said this: 'I have no feeling of confidence.' And he used to say: 'If I come into the room everybody will at once go out of that room.' So he grew sadder, and a poor sort of acquaintance came in numbers to drink the whisky, that was at this time six and sixpence a bottle, and to play whist and to smoke until two o'clock in the morning.

And if your mother and I asked him: 'Shall we go to this place, or to that? Or have these people to dinner, or those?' he would say: 'You must decide for yourselves.' But we were too young to decide wisely. And so your mother met your father and married him. But you must hurry, Celia, surely you will be late at the bureau.

Oh no, Auntie, it isn't nine o'clock yet.

Oh very well, I really do not know why you trouble to go at all and perhaps if you went a little earlier it would not be necessary for you to come home so late at night.

Oh, Auntie, do go on.

I remember, my Aunt went on, often coming out of Christ's Church on a Sunday morning, your grandfather would say: 'Hurry, girls, hurry, and there may be time for a glass of champagne before lunch.'

Champagne, Auntie?

Ah well in those days there was plenty of it, and far from expensive, in fact your grandfather used to have a great many bottles of it given to him, along with some prime venison and some cigars, which he said were not so good as the ones he could buy for himself.

But why did he have them given to him?

Oh, it was something to do with his business, I do not know, it was some sort of present some of the business men would give him, oh no doubt it was for something, but your grandfather always said: 'I will take whatever they care to give me, and it will make no pottle of difference to what I may order or where I may place my orders,' oh, something to do with that, all business. I remember at one time, oh yes, the cellar was so full, and it was so inconvenient, we had it enlarged and we used to keep the bath chair in front of the door, for really there were some times when really if anyone had looked inside, it would have looked rather peculiar, oh rather peculiar—in his position.

But tell me, Auntie, I said, why was my mama so often being sad before she married Papa? Certainly when we were born, my sister and I, and after that, there was some cause for sadness.

Your grandfather, said my Aunt, had no patience with her, he thought she was a peevish, dreamy little girl. 'Oh, you little spitfire,' he would say. But your mother had a more even temper than I, but she was silent when he rounded on her, and grew so sad and dreamy that he could not bear it. Now when he was cross with me, I was also cross with him, and said so, and that he could understand and respect, but your mama would not say one word, but was unhappy and silent. Also, not meaning to be unkind, or indeed pausing one moment to think, he would laugh at her fancies, and he would laugh at the paintings she used to do at school and bring home to show him. And so altogether it was not happy between them.

My Aunt now bustled into the kitchen and came back with a half-sized whisky bottle. Here is your priority milk, she said, now mind you drink it yourself and don't give it to anyone else.

Not even to Raji? I said slyly, for Aunt has a soft spot for my Indian friend.

Well, certainly he looks as if he needs it, poor fellow, said my Aunt, but what is the sense of the doctor giving it to you if you do not drink it? Now you really must be off, really I don't know how they put up with it, have you brushed your hair?

My hair?

Why you must scrag it back like that I do not know, why do you not drape it a little over the forehead?

I tie a handkerchief round my head and knot it under my chin.

No hat? Oh, how I hate those handkerchiefs, they look so unbusinesslike.

I think, I said, that the reason I am often so sad is because I ought not to be in a Ministry at all, I ought to be a North Sea pirate, like my grandfather—a pirate, a pirate, a pirate.

We are all seafaring men in our family, said my Aunt, with complacency, bustling me towards the door. Even your poor father. . . .

When I open my morning paper in the train (the *Telegraph* I leave for my aunt at home), my eye is caught by one of the smaller paragraph headings: it reads 'Old Carthusian Mauled by Japs'. When my Aunt shut the door it was another world and another century. As I step into the Ministry I think, I am now in the world of Carthusians-Etonians-Marlburians-Wykehamists, with Japs upon the threshold and a hundred years set up against my noble elders, my noble Aunt, her noble brother my Uncle Heber. But I can time-skid, if they cannot, I can go to them, if they cannot come to me. I show the paragraph heading to dear Tiny: Look, I say, laughing, look.

What do you know about that? says Tiny, absent-mindedly, slipping vulgarly—a habit he shares with my cousin Caz—into what he supposes to be the accent of our Ally.

Not so much as the Old Carthusian, I say coldly.

Tiny looked at the paper again. And how many Japs have been mauled by Old Carthusians, do you suppose?

There is a note on my desk to say that Harley will be in for lunch. Harley is my immediate superior officer at the Ministry, and for him I often do some special work. He is passing backwards and forwards from the Admiralty to the Ministry, he is Admiralty Liaison.

I now went out and bought some chocolate for him. And I went over to Lopez's and had some morning coffee with her in the garden. And Lopez told me about her B.B.C. interviews, and of the great things that are in train, and how Marjorie never finishes a sentence, but says: 'There must be a new, there must be, you see, it is not.'

And the sun streamed down into the little Chelsea garden, and later Lopez walked back with me to the bus stop. And though I could not tell Lopez at all why I was so sad, and how I was so sad, it was a happy thing to be near her and with her; she is so unlike me at this moment, she is very flip.

Then I come back to the Ministry, and I lie down upon the floor of the lavatory and stare up at the ceiling where the plaster has been shaken off. I feel absolutely ghost-girl deficient. Ah, how much it tears.

There is a pounding on the door.

Who is it? I cry.

Oh, it's you, Celia, it's me, Constance, oh do hurry up, what ages you take, I must finish that Report for Jacky, it simply can't wait, I haven't a minute, oh do hurry up.

Harley comes in at one-thirty. We have lunch together in the Planners' Room. Mrs. Bones, the Housekeeper, gives us stewed steak, potatoes, carrots, cabbage, rice pudding and treacle.

I did not want to talk to Harley to-day, so I found two copies of *Esquire*, and I read one and he read the other. There was this friendly silence. I said: If you see somebody doing the work they like doing, doing it well, going on doing it, and earning enough to live upon, you can hardly believe your eyes.

Harley said: How is Aunt Tiger?

(My Aunt is like a lion and so we call her sometimes Aunt Lion.)

It is lion, I say.

Harley began to talk about a canary he is thinking of buying.

As I washed up the lunch things in cold water, as we have turned off the hot water to save the heating, I thought: Shall I ever be rid of this misery, is it papa's legacy, or my mama's, or is it the war, or is it the guilt of our social situation that is so base bottom bad? This sneering situation that is built on money.

When I was talking to Tom one day, when he was in his good mood and talking freely, he said we were about due

42

for a religious revival, and I said: O yes, there were already signs of it. And I told him I had recently been sent in for review *Grey Eminence*, *Screwtape Letters* and *Death and Life* by Father D'Arcy.

Well, said Tom, how did it go?

Well, I said, to begin with I felt exalted and relieved, to begin with the Christian solution seemed the one. Especially in *Eminence*, I thought, there is much to encourage. But then it fell away from me, it turned to exasperation. Tom, I said, it too much bears the mark of our humanity, this Christian religious idea, it is too tidy, too tidy by far. In its extreme tidy logic it is a diminution and a lie. These rewards and punishments, this grading, this father-son-teacher-pupil idea, it too much bears the human wish for something finished off and tidy, something one can grasp lovingly and tight, trusting to the Father, the Son and the Holy Ghost. It is the most tearing and moving thing, this wish to gain marks and approval, to plod on, with personal and loving chastisement, to infinity. This beating idea is also something that is always coming up. The truth is that people cannot bear not to be beaten.

I read Father D'Arcy's book in proof, said Tom. When I had finished it I said: I don't believe a word of it.

We both began to laugh.

It cannot be like this, I said, it is not possible.

V

THIS WEEK-END I have been out with Tiny and with his brother Clem. Lopez will not come because she does not like the company of her brothers and also because she is reluctant to put one foot in front of the other. Lopez is a flat-bound girl; she is fat, and stays indoors.

Clem is terribly malicious. He is older than Tiny by six minutes, so it is he who has the title. He is enormously rich, he is the worst type of rich person. He is a small sly fat beast, playing left wing politics but looking out for number one.

As we sit under the lee of a haystack, to keep our sandwiches dry from the thin rain that is beginning to fall, he tells us, or rather he tells me, since Tiny is glum and dissociates himself from the conversation, he tells me about the time just before the war when he was at Istamboul.

But you are not listening, Celia, he says spreading his fat fingers in mock resignation, I fear I am a sad bore.

I do wish Tiny would wake up, I say, Tiny, what are you thinking about, where are you?

Tiny does not reply, but goes on staring glumly at the wet hens that are fidgeting round us, pecking at the corn cobs.

Tiny should be interested, said Clem, with a nasty look at his little brother: Do you not remember, Tiny, when you came out to stay with us at Istamboul, I said at Istamboul, my dear chap? It was there you know—he turned to me

44

with a cat whisper that was perfectly audible to Tiny—it was there that he first met Vera Hennessey, eh Tiny?

Oh do shut up, said Tiny.

Vera is rather a stiff proposition you know, said Clem, Tiny used to take her sailing on the Bosphorus, they used to start off without saying a word, I don't believe Vera *ever* said a word, she used to sit there, rather a touching little thing really, with her great black eyes and that *air d'enfant abusé* mixed up with the *femme fatale*, of course that was really her line, and she had enough sense to keep her mouth shut. . . .

Oh how I wish you would, groaned Tiny.

How sharp he is. Vera's mama was Turkish you know, and Vera rather cultivated the manner of her mother's people, there was something really rather piquantly out of date about the whole thing, it was so much the Turkey of Abdul the Damned, you know, Vera was very Pierre Loti in her adherence to the ramshackle Ottoman Empire, in dress, in appearance, above all in that wistful submissive positively trampled silence. Of course she is not at all submissive really, as poor Hennessey has probably learnt to his cost by this time, but in those days she affected the manner, at once *peureuse et soumise*, that one associates—Clem lowered his voice—with the inmates of certain houses, whose wages, poor girls, always seem to be deducted at source *in toto*.

O do shut up, said Tiny.

Of course that was the trouble, she really wanted to be raped.

Oh do shut up.

And we know how disobliging Tiny can be.

Later she became a papist and used to talk in the most intimate way about—again the shivering whisper by way of emphasis, and a most unnecessary glance over his shoulder to make sure that we were not overheard—*Our Lord*

I remember that story of Pierre Loti's, I said, rushing rather feebly I fear to the rescue of poor Tiny, at least I do remember that there were these sad harem ladies who were always rushing out of the harem, wrapped up all over in black clothes and looking like postage bundles, and taking a cab and galloping in this cab until they came to the shores of the Bosphorus where in a cemetery bordering the sea-walk. . . .

> Where in a garden of dedicated roses,
>   (Clem interrupted me.)
> Oft did a priestess, as lovely as a vision,
> Pouring her soul to the son of Cytherea,
> Pray him to hover above the slight canoe boat,
> And with invisible pilotage to guide it
> Over the dusky seas, until the nightly singer
> Shivering with ecstasy sank upon her bosom.

No, I said, where there was the French author waiting for them. So then the ladies would pay off the *cocher* and tell him to call again in an hour and a half, and oh how chilly the east wind drew from off the stormy sea, and so, gathering their clothes about them they made off to the tombstones, and there, sheltering with the French author behind the tombstone, while the cypress waved melancholy in the wind, they would eat their sandwiches and sip their sherbert, and they would have these fascinating long talks with the sympathetic Frenchman, these doctrinaire advanced discussions about the position of women, and all the time the tears for their plight was frozen on their cheeks by reason of . . . .

The east wind, said Clem, firmly. He squeezed the water out of his scarf, which had fallen into a puddle, and cast his eyes aloft: I'm not at all sure that we shouldn't make for that barn, just now that the rain is not raining so fast.

46

We made no move.

We're as much out of it as in it, said Tiny, who looked as frozen cold blue and miserable as the beastly Bosphorus.

But now the rain suddenly stopped and the warm sunshine fell upon the ground and began to lap up the moisture; to the north the sky was a beautiful sapphire blue, but over to the west the storm clouds massed in angry greys and purples; the grass was a beautiful bright dark green where the sunshine lay upon it, up against where the angry shadow of the stormclouds fell.

We got up, shook the crumbs off us, and began to walk again.

Clem looked appreciatively upon the scenery and cracked his fingers. One always comes back to the English School, he said.

The country road was a beautiful ochre speckled with blue-grey gravel. It meandered along at a higher level than the fields, so that we could see the fields and the woods falling away from us across the low hedges. In the distance were the blue Hertfordshire-Cambridgeshire hills, on our right was a fine landed estate that had first fallen into the hands of a preparatory school: but now on its gateposts of a country gentleman were scrawled the W.D.'s of our time.

Clem, mindful of his figure, lapped ahead at a good pace, but Tiny and I walked together slowly. We did not talk. I took poor Tiny's hand and he gave my hand a mild squeeze.

It can be bitterly cold by the Bosphorus, he said.

When we came home from our trip in the country, Clem said: Our darling looks pale, come in and lie down for a few moments.

Clem is a notable b——. Clem is married, his wife lives in a country place, she does not come to London or attend the parties. The two daughters are called Glory and Selwyn, they are at the highclass boarding school of Redesdale St. Mary, where my sister is teaching. Selwyn and Glory are in her division, she teaches the two girls Greek and Latin. One day Selwyn lay down on the floor and she would not move, she said: If I lie here for a time then I shall be dead, that is what I wish.

Selwyn said she could not tolerate her father, but that when he came home she must sit on his knee and pretend that she loved him dearly. She said it was expected. Selwyn told me this herself, sitting on a bank above the swift river that runs by the school estate. When Selwyn was four somebody met her running along the road, running very fast.

Where are you off to, Selwyn? they asked.

Selwyn said, I am going to take lodgings.

Glory finds herself more easily at home. In the park you will say: Have you enjoyed your walk, Glory? And Glory will look in an affected way at her nurse, and she will say: Did we enjoy our walk, Nanny? well rather yes perhaps rather.

These are the daughters of the b——, and this is the life in the family.

Running up the steps of Tiny's house with my arm crooked in his, I say, Tiny, your brother is a notable b——. He should have these words on his gravestone: Here lies a notable b——.

Tiny sits beside me on the couch. He says: Do you remember the beige cows that were coming behind the water towers?

We have been for this favourite walk in the country. There is this water tower and these beige cows that have always attracted Tiny, they have neat coats lying close to the body without a fold, they are animals with delicate feet, their coats are this beige colour which Tiny likes so much.

I know that Tiny is waiting to tell me about Vera Hennessey, he is now leading up to have a love talk about Vera. But my mood has swung over to the mood of the wretched Clem, for whom the most that can be said is that he has now gone off to his own place and is no longer with us.

I hurry up to say something to make a pause.

I say—it is what I have read in the papers—the new type of British Consular Officer is a man of wide culture and knowledge. Often he has missed the Diplomatic Service by a few marks only. Did you know?

Yes . . . (*C'est mal réussi, ça.*)

I lie back and feel rather bored. He knows everything in a little way, and thinks of Vera. Does your cat leap? Maybe he has fits. The cats and the beige cows are already floating away upon the mirage of the desert of love.

Tiny says: Do you ever feel so cold, so frozen cold, so far away, and that love is a desperate chance clutch upon a hen-coop in mid-Atlantic?

Oh yes, Tiny, I say, kissing him, I do often feel like this.

At the station this morning, I say, there were two dancing boys on their way to ballet-class. One said to the other, 'I think she has rather a sullen personality.' 'Oh no,' said the other, 'she is not really a sullen personality; her mother you know is in a lunatic asylum.' So perhaps you see we do what we can, it is perhaps this inherited tendency. Or something. But oh, Tiny, if death is not the end, then indeed there is no hope. 'Dost thou see the precipice? . . .' I do not think that Seneca would have spoken so glibly if he had had the Christian idea. But oh, oh, this sadness stops everything, it stops writing, for it comes out so much in that, and it stops anything but the most sketchy of the love-sex idea.

Tiny, I said, I think that man is composed of three things.

49

There is the man, I said, and the cards he is playing, and there is a man watching over his shoulder.

And the cards are the fate, and the player is the life, and the watcher is the spirit. Yes, this Watcher is a bit of an enigma. Perhaps he is the *Weltgeist*. So then it is like a dream, it shifts, and the player and the cards vanish, but in their place there is now a stream that is made of two parts, that mix together, that make a food mixture. But the spirit is there, and he is hungry. So he stoops and drinks of that food mixture. And now he is no longer hungry.

He is smooth? said Tiny.

Yes, I said, very smooth and grim.

Tiny, I say, casting him a malicious look, for suddenly he is looking like his brother. Yes, in that pale sad Plantagenet face that is so close to mine there is very much the look of brother Clem, so frivolous and deathly, that will mop and mow and dress its fat body in fancy dress, and be so deathly. So, Tiny, I cry, listen, Tiny, love is everything, it is the only thing, one looks for it. Yes, everybody is hankering after it and whining. This hunger we have is a good thing, it is the long shin bone that shows the child will grow tall.

Tiny rocked himself backwards and forwards.

The growing, he said, is very painful, it is like the Princess walking upon pins and needles.

Dear Tiny, I say, and kiss him again. Tiny, I say, I had a curious dream last night. It was very vivid, I sigh. I was in a room with a lot of people, and my sister came in. I had kept her waiting, she was very cross. So afterwards I was walking down a street with her, and I said (it was the cruellest thing I could say), why are you so cross, Pearl, so *farouche*? You behaved like an animal, you were like an animal. At this moment we were passing a cinema. So my sister said, in the most gentle way imaginable, so very gently:

'Let us go in here.' And there were two programmes billed on two separate posters. And one was called 'Mr. Hardman and Mr. Wallace will be Happier when They have Left the Young People'. And the other was 'Amphitryon III'.

I pressed my face down against his knee. This is terrible, I said. Then I said cruelly: This love we were speaking of has nothing to do with Vera Hennessey.

Tiny and I felt warmer for our conversation, and later we made some coffee and got down to the figures we had to work out for the Ministry people. Seven-eight cross to two-four, it was that sort of thing.

I am very happy when I am working, and so is Tiny, we work very cleverly and quickly. Then why do you not always work hard and so forget your beastly unhappiness? Oh well, that is just to say, I am happy when I am unconscious.

The next day at the Ministry I type out my review of the book *Boethius* by Miss Helen Barret, that is for the Department of Civilian Morale.

This is what I have written.

'Boethius was a Roman Philosopher who lived in sixth-century Italy. He saw his country overrun by the barbarians and Rome "captured that had taken captive all the world". The barbarian leader was a brave and energetic man called Theodoric. He did not wish to destroy Italy, as Alaric the Hun would have done, but to preserve and strengthen everything that was good in Roman rule. He governed wisely and promoted to office the best men among the Romans. It was Theodoric who drew Boethius away from his studies and made him Master of Offices, that is to say something like Foreign Secretary, Home Secretary and Postmaster-General rolled into one.

'His duties left Boethius little time for philosophy, but he brought to his new tasks something of that donnish obstinacy and cocksureness which makes people difficult to get on with. It was an age of famous squabbles. The Bishops of Rome and Constantinople had just excommunicated each other in the Church of St. Sophia. Boethius too had his squabbles. He made enemies because he was reckless in exposing his colleagues' weaknesses—especially a tendency here and there to divert public funds to private uses.

'Theodoric's Finance Minister, Cyprian, began to be nervous about this; he resented anyone poking his nose into the Exchequer; he remembered perhaps that Boethius had also written a treatise on arithmetic. So he decided to poke his nose into the affairs of the Postmaster-General and he intercepted letters from Boethius to the Emperor in Constantinople. He put his own construction on these letters and persuaded Theodoric that there was a plot on foot to drive the Goths out of Italy. Boethius was charged with treason and thrown into jail under sentence of death.

'He was not very philosophic about this. He said that the accusation was false—which it almost certainly was—and that the accusers were the sort of people who would be glad to liquidate their debts by perjury, which seems unlikely, at least in the case of the Finance Minister, who had other sources of relief. However, prison life gave Boethius time to get on with his studies, and before he was executed he wrote his most famous book—*The Consolation of Philosophy*. It is about good and evil, and justifies the ways of God to man, and shows that though the wicked may do very well for themselves in this world, they are not really happy because they are bad. Cyprian, for instance, might grow fat on peculation, but he was not really so happy as Boethius, though it might look otherwise to the profane, seeing that Boethius was under sentence of torture and death.

'*The Consolation of Philosophy* is not a book for good men in reduced circumstances only, it has a wider appeal. King Alfred thought the world of it, so did Geoffrey Chaucer, Queen Elizabeth and Edward Gibbon. It tries to solve the ancient problems of free will and pain and eternity. And there is something humanly heroic in the way the book came to be written—human because of Boethius's despair and indignation at his unjust treatment, and heroic because he got the better of his feelings and not only found, but handed on to others, consolation in philosophy.'

As I read this through I begin to ponder and feel hopeful. Boethius is the sort of person one can admire. Boethius took public office high up, he operated with integrity in situations of horror and depression and from a full heart of black experience he wrote his book.

One wishes also to be admirable, to write something that is truly noble, but the times are wrong, they are certainly wrong, at least in the West they are wrong. And there are too many words, there is too much about it and about, one has this horror of words—'I'll be dumb'—but no, one must not be dumb. Somebody should speak up.

In Russia, we are told, there is this simplicity and single-mindedness that is so noble and so admirable, they have not been touched by the weakening and destroying civilisation of the West, they are not corrupt. And believing or half-believing this idea about Russia, we feel guilty and are irritable. It is that thought about a thought that nags at us, and we seem to do nothing but a lot of things that are nothing. For we are not prepared to give up our way of life, for we have no bloody revolution since three hundred years, for we have this disgusting temporising mind, we will give up a little but not everything, we will pare away a little here and there, we will make accommodations with conscience, but all the time, No, we will not give up our Western way, indeed we will not, why we cannot conceive of such a thing, not really to imagine it. And Government sees to it that the majority of the people shall have a stake in our civilization, they shall have a qualifying Judas one-pound share.

And why should we give it up, pray, and in what way is it a Judas stake, eh? And what is this nonsense about Russia? Is Russia such a pretty country, does it smell so sweet; is it not corrupt? (Is it civilized?) So we swing round again and cry out upon the truth and the half-truth: Lies, lies, lies. It is the slough of the war and the post-war that is sucking us in, yes, certainly, it is the Devil of the Meridian, it is the devil of a middle situation that has us by the throat, it is the *trahison des clercs*. So that is how it is and we are rightly wretched. Courage, we should rather cry: Work in silence for the time to pass.

When Caz was on Intelligence in Berlin he said that the Russian soldiers were like children, they had not before seen anything like Berlin, they came to stare and to destroy. But suddenly they would be so happy and they would run suddenly mad, and if they could lay hands on a car that could do so much, then they would tear at a hundred miles an hour along the autobahn, and there would be the driver, and half a dozen men inside the car, and another half a dozen hanging on the running board, and another half a dozen biting the roof of it to hang on by their teeth; and so they would go, with a tra la la and Off for the day; and heaven help the rest of the allied traffic along that autobahn. Why one day, Caz said, he was keeping a lap ahead by the grace of God and a Rolls Royce engine, and by and by they came to the U.S.A. post that was about to stand them all up for a paper count. So 'Let me through, pal,' yelled Caz, 'I've got a Comrade on my heels.' So the Yank let him through and dropped the barrier, and the Comrades, who couldn't stop, turned off into a field to avoid the post, and round and round spun the car that they couldn't stop, and off fell the comrades in a holiday mood, and no one was hurt.

Caz said that the Russian soldiers looked at the German girls and they said, 'Gom, Frau,' which was all they knew of the German language and all they needed to know. And the poor shivering Frau would creep up to the Comrade like a little rabbit to be devoured, and devoured she would be with a vengeance, and all in a holiday mood.

These travellers' tales lift the dark mood, I love to hear the travellers' tales and the tales of the soldiers who come home. I asked the soldier what had happened to the animals in the jungles of Burma, for this was a thing that I wished to know: Well, what happened to the jungle animals in all the fighting and scurrying of the armies, well, did the animals flee, did they clear out, the animals and the reptiles, did they quit, did they move off to another jungle? 'Oh no,' said the young soldier, 'the animals stayed, they were another worry, just something more for us to have. The tigers used to bite our men and they used to eat the Japanese, and the crocs used to nab a chap every now and then, and the monkeys were very mischievous. But the tigers were the worst, they were the limit.' My soldier from the wars returning said: 'Crumbs, what with the Japs, the jungle, the animals and the Beds and Herts (that was his regiment), crumbs, it was indeed a circus.'

When I am walking with Lopez along the King's Road I keep close to her for company. Here is this admirable girl, I think, who has this admirable courage and this admirable high heart, for she is not a sad girl, she is not walking round

55

in fury and despair. She writes and entertains the Government and the Section people, and the editors, and all the time it is nothing but a wonderful adventure for her to have, it is in the spirit of the Scarlet Pimpernel, or Sideways Through Patagonia, it is like that. Oh vigorous buccaneering delicate girl-o, what a wonderful girl Lopez is, she is the divine Helen to the Castor and Pollux of her rather undivine brothers, I think, walking home with her along the King's Road.

Another day at the Ministry is over, I am one day nearer to my holiday, I am one day nearer to that blessed calm Heber and to my cousin.

I am still thinking about Boethius, who had his own problems of contacts and self-establishment (lest a worse man should get the job) in a corrupt society, and I tell Lopez what happened when I went to the Book Prints Exhibition that the Ministry is holding. The first person I saw there (I tell Lopez) was Raji. Do you happen to notice, I said, that the Queen is standing next to you? Raji said, I think this King-Queen business is sad. We stood on the first floor landing to watch the Queen walk below. We could have poured sherry in her hat. Raji said that throughout England there is this dummy-power idea. There is the King, but of course since a long time it is not the King who pulls the shower bath. And in the Civil Service, and in the City, and in the Ministries and in Publishing, it is the same, the power hides and works and pulls the shower bath.

But oh, Lopez, I said, in this idea of Raji's that we are treading a secret hell, that we are weeping in the peasoup fog of a secret power, that we can do nothing but cough and snore a little in our throats, and so go out into the darkness, in this idea there is the poison of a beastly self-pity. And it can attack the vigorous as the weak.

56

And of this we were at once to have a reminder. For when we got back to Lopez's house and were having our tea, a famous writer arrived, an old pink man, looking like a baby, in a hooded cloak.

Kiss me, Lopez, he said, with his arms around beautiful fat Lopez. And then he said: Now you kiss me, Celia.

Oh, how can I do that, I said, you will have the lipstick all over your face.

What, he said, do you use lipstick? And you've got sich an innercint fice.

But this famous writer's books are still hitting the note of self-pity for the days when he served shop—'my bankrupt boyhood'. Self-pity is the devil. But the old chap is in good form this evening and instructs us—misinstructs us I rather think—upon the political situation. We sit at his feet, making toast for him, gazing up at him with bright eyes and fire-flushed cheeks. Lopez's fat cat, that she has borrowed from the writer to get rid of her mice, lies upon the lower shelf of the tea-trolly and hangs his fat large head close against the fire; he is in the ecstasy of being about to be too hot. We beam generously upon the old frail one—oh sir, oh sir, oh I say, Sir—it is rather that note. We are his young ones, his instructed. He thinks that we are children and believe every word that he says.

VI

WHEN I GET home, to my own home, to my
suburb, my sister is there, she has just arrived from
Northumberland, she is happy (my sister Pearl is a school
teacher). Pearl is happy in this new school she has been at
now for one half-term.

My sister was not always so happy in her schools. In her
last school, it was in Wales, it was like a madhouse. There
it was a mixed boy-girl school, with a young, diffident and
obstinate headmaster. He thought that to do the wrong thing
strongly is better than to do nothing, but only he was by
nature so vacillating that he could not even make up his
mind what was the wrong thing, but if he was not impeded
by a rationalizing attempt, he would do the wrong thing
with a splendid spontaneity.

The female sub-head in this school was a super thyroid
who screamed and cried and made everybody so nervous.
When the poor child was sick, she said: 'You cannot be
sick here.' But where could he be sick? He was driven into
the cold playground where the rain fell.

In the commercial class the little boy wrote a business
letter: 'Sadly we see our customers falling away from us,
but I hope that we shall always be friends. And so, with
love.' But soon he was taught the business language, ah
that one was not quite the business language, but soon he was
corrected.

This school building had been condemned since a long time by the education committee. But the local council had the idea to keep expenses down, they were proud of their renown in this endeavour, they were indeed the cheapest in the kingdom for school rates.

So then the war comes, and of course nothing can be done.

And all the time the children were being whipped. And Pearl thought it might be possible to whip the Harrow children and the Eton children, who are well fed, fat, and have a social security, but that it should not be possible to whip poor thin boys who are hungry, no, that should not be possible, because it breaks them up, they cannot bear it, it has destroyed them.

During the war the little children of this condemned school sat for many days in the damp air-raid shelters, for in that part of the country, it was near a great west coast sea-port, the raids were very frequent. And the children's cloakrooms were often awash with rain water, and they could not change their shoes; they got real ill. And they were crammed for scholarships and tormented, though it was (the young schoolmaster thought) for their own good.

There was also the little boy that his parents wished to get a scholarship for Eton, so Pearl must coach him in Greek. He got meningitis, he is now dead.

This was a bad school, with so much hatred between the teachers, and I-don't-see-why-I-should-do-it and he-says and she-says.

Pearl became ill with bronchitis, perhaps it was a saving bit of psychology that did it. It was the end of that school for her, she came home.

Now she is at this high-class boarding school of Redesdale St. Mary, but she sighs for the children of the other school because she says they were so quick and could have quickly understood so much, but it was not possible, they were always tired, and the homes not good. But these fat little rich girls, they are not so quick, but sweet, too, and hard working and loving. But they are growing big girls and are kept children.

An old school friend of mine, called Olive, came down with me for a week-end to stay with Pearl and to see the school. Very grand it was, with the rich Italianate pictures that was an eighteenth century parvenu's collection and a safe bet. They were starred with stars, one, two or three stars for priority in salvage, in case of incendiary bombs.

But, I said, surely that cannot be a genuine Titian? for it has no stars on it at all.

This house, and the pictures in it, belong to Clem. Clem has let it out for this school to have.

We went all over the house and we climbed up through the attics and climbed on to the roof and walked around and looked upon the river and we saw the great limestone cliff, where Clem's great grandfather threw himself down, and so died, and Clem might do worse.

Olive and I stayed at the house of the Misses Bird. This was an old-fashioned pair. The elder was all smiles and chat, but the younger could only hang her head and blush. They were ladies of sixty. The tea they brought us had a real wild flavour, and Olive, I said, just lift up the lid and have a look. So she did, and coiled up at the bottom of the pot was a blue bag which had tea in it, and it was not the first time that tea had been boiled, no, not by a long chalk.

Pearl came to breakfast with us after she had been to mass. She is a Roman Catholic, though brought up as I am in the anglican fold. But it was the prayer book controversy that did it, that sent her off. But she is happy, in the religion at least she is happy, though of crocodile birth with me, she cannot be altogether happy, of course that is not possible. She knocked at the door, and I went, and she began to cry.

Oh, Pearl, what is it, darling? I said, and began to cry too. For everything has now gone wrong for Pearl. The priest did not arrive for one hour later, the cows outside her billet had cried all the early morning, and everything was bitter as salt water, and black. We stood in the hall crying softly. Oh, how different is this love for relations from the love for friends. Oh, how it strains and tears.

But when Pearl becomes miserable she also becomes cross, it is the fighting temperament she has, and everything now becomes her enemy. The bicycle is her enemy, the newly gravelled road, the terrible Miss Harrison, the farm billet.

So instead of the rich death-feeling that is what I have, that is so richly anarchic and upon which one can rest, she has this furious feeling of earthly rage. So this makes her a difficult companion; it is perhaps better to rest upon the black waters.

Olive is a calm girl, enjoying a private income and no cares.

After lunch at this school I was very tired. I laid my coat by the side of the rhododendron bushes and fell asleep. When I woke up Olive said: You are like a dog, you lie down and go to sleep after a meal, you are like a dog, you are three inches more round the waist and go to sleep.

But I was thinking: Oh shall we ever get through life, oh, when will it be over? But first must come old age, with the mind stuck in creaking joints and hardening arteries. O mors, quam amara est memoria tua. . . . I cannot agree.

I turned restlessly, pressing my stomach upon the soft beautiful grass, to repent of these wolfish words, to ask forgiveness. There is such an air of innocence about this soft grass and the great mild parkland, and the ancient soft trees, and the great stone that lies upon the grass, and the feather fronds of the summer bracken that I look up at over my head, and the dark green leaves of the rhododendron trees, that the happiness floods into my heart, the usual great happiness. Oh what is the barrier that stands out against this happiness, and what are the wolfish words upon our lips that deny it, the words that are not our words? What is the dog within us that howls against it, the dog that tears and howls, that is no creature of ours, that lies within, kennelled and howling, that is an alien animal, an enemy? It is the desire to tear out this animal, to have our heart free of him, to have our heart for ourselves and for the innocent happiness, that makes us cry out against life, and cry for death. For this animal is kennelled close within, and tearing out this animal we tear out also the life with it.

> I'll have thy heart, if not by gift my knife
> Shall carve it out, I'll have thy heart, thy life.

When I was talking to Harley at the Ministry one day about my poems, he said, I am rather disturbed about this death feeling in your poems.

Oh, I said, that is nothing, that death feeling, it is absolutely nothing.

Harley is this Liaison with Admiralty. At the Ministry there is also Rackstraw. He is much older than Harley. He is Inside Relations. But there is also a third man I have to do with. He is St. John. So my life at the Ministry is rather difficult in this triangular way. For St. John is the one. Yes, it is St. John who does all the work, and shoulders the responsibility, and he is one of the Planners, and that is indeed the top.

St. John is an austere hardworking creature, whereas Harley and Rackstraw are rather the boys in Pop. Now St. John does not mind Rackstraw, because Rackstraw is this sweet-tempered old gentleman, the sweetest-tempered old gentleman in the world. Everybody loves Rackstraw, but it is different with Harley. St. John does not love Harley, he does not understand Harley's casual conversation, there is indeed not much love lost between the two of them.

One day I was lunching with Clem. And Clem said: Guess what I had for breakfast, guess what breakfast fruit I had, and I will give you one pound.

So I said: Mangosteen.

You're right, he said, it was a mango, and he slapped down a pound note on the tablecloth.

Mind you, I said, I'm not saying mangosteen is the same as mango.

At four o'clock that afternoon Clem rang me on the inter-com.

Celia, he said, mangosteen isn't the same as mango, so you will have to give me the pound back, won't you, dear, I mean it's no use keeping it, dear, if it isn't, is it?

So at that moment Harley came in from the Admiralty, and I asked him what I should do.

If you are a purist, he said, you will have to give it back, but I do not know how much of a purist you are. On the other hand you can keep it and ask him out to lunch. But as Clem is such a vindictive fellow, he will be sure to eat more than one pound's worth, with no effort at all he will do this.

Was I not fortunate to associate with so bland and discreet a person as Harley? Was I not fortunate in this?

Why should I set so high the good opinion of that other one, that old devil St. John? I will tell you. St. John was

63

once curate to my Uncle Heber in the East End of London. St. John respects Heber, as Heber does him.

In my diary that night I wrote: I guess I am damned, the wickedness in my heart is something radical.

This morning I was feeling so distraught about the difficulties of having a lot to do with all the different people at the Ministry, with Harley, Rackstraw, and St. John, with Clem and Tiny, with Eleanor and Constance, with the little messenger girl, and the girls and the men I see only on my night shift evenings, and I was feeling how truly difficult and absorbing people are; and now Jacky Sparrow sent me very urgently a book about apes to cut down for a broadcast talk. And this book said how the American lady who wrote the book kept a zooful of gibbons, orang-utans ('the men of the woods'), and chimpanzees and gorillas, and how dearly she loved them.

And there stood the great ape, photographed upon the dust wrapper, there he stood in his shaggy coat, standing on his hind legs to look with such a loving look at his kind mistress, and the lady's face was close to the ape's face, and there was the animal barrier between them, and yet affection and trust.

And this lady said how the apes were bossy and moody and jealous and wild, and yet uncomplicated by trying to be something else. Yet in the dark eyes of that animal was real fondness. And I thought: It is not so difficult for them, but we have come further than the apes and know what we are and do not like it and want to be something else. And I thought: We have come some way from the apes, but we think we have not come fast enough or far enough, and so fall into abuse and despair. But looking at the violent dark creature that is one step down from us, I cried out to Harley: There is nothing I can do for you, there is nothing at all, I should go, that is all that I should do. And I thought, we are born of an age of unrest, and unrestful we are, with a vengeance.

The idea is to go, go, go. Go from the apes, from Harley, from the friends.

So that evening I went to sit with Lopez, and I sat in her sitting room colouring some of my drawings, and I was telling her about the Ministry, and about the great ones, the Harley, the Rackstraw and the St. John, and about the lesser ones, and about the truly ape-like difficulties of friendships, and about the jealousies, the ferocity, the cruelty of a couple of she-friends I have in mind, where the one will play cat-and-mouse and the other will play doormat, and yet they love each other truly and cannot part.

I suppose they will kill each other in the end, I said, and I laughed: It is all for love. And yet, I went on, I could not have imagined a friendship between girls where it could have mattered, it must be a nervous situation, it has to be that.

What is that you are singing, Celia, said Lopez.

Oh, it is just that thing Raji was singing at your party, about the Suttee lady and what she was thinking.

Lopez said: My brother had a friendship with a poet, it was a friendship you know, he was not getting off with the poet. Stop singing now, Celia. I used to think it was such nonsense, this friendship. I cannot understand why one bothers really, not altogether understand.

But people do bother, I said, in friendship as in love, they do bother. Nothing that produces suffering can be nothing, and friendship does produce suffering, so it cannot be absolutely nothing.

When one is out of it . . ., said Lopez.

Or when it is running smoothly, I said, for nothing irks one more than opposition.

Yes, then one looks at the poor dark sufferers and only wishes to slap them.

There was a man I once had a fancy for, dear old C., always so quiet you know, and he made me laugh so much. Friendship should be a pleasant reliable thing with conversation. Do you like intellectual conversation?

I do not shy away from it like you do, you are absolutely non-conductive to opinions.

Oh, that is the worst sort of conversation. I like chat awfully. The best conversation is gossip and folly. Love is adorable, I say, and anger too. When a child is basely treated for the first time, he knows for the first time the extremity of anger; he wishes to kill. When peace comes again, he looks back with longing to that violent moment. I adore the emotions.

And also I suppose, said Lopez, you adore death, that is the end of the emotions.

As we are sitting talking, a shadow blows across the sun and the wind is blowing up cold from the river. I put my hands to my face and lean back against the wall. I wish that my cousin Casmilus was here to fetch me away, and that my holiday, that does not start until next week, was already here.

Lopez says: You are married to Death and Hades; all my friends are married to Death and Hades.

Lopez went off to see a man who had called about the telephone, and Basil Tait and Tom Fox came in. They had been standing on the doorstep trying to make somebody hear.

Basil began talking about when he was fighting in Spain.

He said that in Madrid there was the street fighting going on, and the machine-guns at the street corners, and the light tanks running around; and all the time that this was happening the Serenas (that is the porters they have at the big flat-blocks) were walking up and down and calling out, 'Two o'clock and a fine night and everything is peaceful', because that was what they had always done, and they would go on doing it.

Tom said: Hallo, Celia, I saw our cousin just now.

You saw Casmilus? I said, oh (for I thought he had gone to the north). Oh yes, I said, and how was it?

Tom looked at me with hostility. He seemed in a hurry, he said. (And then he began to sing, 'Oh who shall beguile us, Like darling Casmilus' in a sneering voice. This was a rhyme we used to plague Caz with when we were all children; but not in a sneering voice.)

Oh? Well, yes, he is very busy just now. It is very cold to-night, I said.

Basil knelt down and put a match to the fire. There was this icy feeling coming out of Tom, but Basil inclined to conversation. He said that very soon the population would be only forty million. He said that the cruelty of the Germans was nothing to what the cruelty of the English would be if the English were really up against it in the matter of losing their property, that is their goods and their money and a chance for the kids.

But all the time that Basil was speaking he was watching Tom. I thought: Basil loves only Tom; Tom is his dear one, his mate, his friend, he is his D. H. Lawrence of a David-and-Jonathan situation; and I felt a contempt for this, and for this hysteria of a masculine *agape* that runs through our English literature and through our life too—'They told me, Heraclitus, they told me you were dead' ... 'The Danube

67

to the Severn gave'.... It is not entirely a homosexual thing (and not entirely not); it is innocent so far as it goes, but innocent?—but juvenile. There is this juvenility that curls the lip of the observer and draws back the cruel smile. 'Farewell, thou art too dear for my possessing'... 'And added one thing to my purpose nothing'? Not quite so innocent that perhaps. Let us turn to the breezier Belloc—no, no, leave it.

Well, that is how it is with Basil. Basil thinks 'the clasp of manly hand in manly friendship'.... Ha, ha, again the unkind smile, the light sneer fleeting upon the countenance of the light god, to whom these boys—well, are they not boys indeed?—make such unsuitable vows. Ha, ha, ha, the laughter echoes through the close oak wood, the oak leaves crown the guilty brow, the boys kneel, the god laughs, passes, draws them after him. The path he draws them upon grows steeper, it is overgrown with brambles and strewn with boulders. The impetuous following feet of the ageing boys bleed against the thorns and are bruised by the stones; their footsteps err. But still the divine delinquent skips merrily ahead, ever young and ever false. The boys' hyacinthine locks by the way are growing rather thin by this time, and those soft eyes of theirs, once dewey-wet, are now scaled with gum. But innocent? Oh I suppose innocent enough.

Basil loves Tom, he does not care for women, he loves only Tom. He thinks that women are biologically necessary and resents the necessity, he is like a twelve-year-old boy, he thinks 'girls are no good'. But he loves this cousin of mine, this Tom, Basil loves him (oh, in the way of friendship, in the way of friendship, he is not getting off with the fellow, oh, no offence in the world). Why the matter between them is plainly to be seen, it is to be seen in the face which is turned upon Tom, in the blue eyes that grow so mild, admiring and happy; oh, happy Basil in his love for his dear one (ah, friendship).

I fancy Tom knows nothing of it, can in fact know nothing of anything but Tom. So that is how it is, I think, and wonder that I never thought of it before, and wonder if Lopez knows, and suppose that she does.

I said that it was the middle classes who would fight to the last ditch for the public schools and the privilege idea because they were so nearly about to clasp it and so nearly about to send the kids to Eton. And I told Basil about Jacky Sparrow at the Ministry, who is this lunching pal of mine, and quite a genial chap, except when it came to the idea of socialism, and the idea of not sending the kids to Eton.

Tom picked a copy of *The Fairchild Family* from the bookshelf and settling himself in the best armchair began to read.

Basil said that eventually England would have to choose between money and kids, because under capitalism people would not have kids, it was too much to ask, and he began to inveigh against our ex-Ally which put me for once in a good humour with them. He said that America would be the ruin of the moral order, he said that the more gadgets women had and the more they thought about their faces and their figures, the less they wanted to have children, he said that he happened to see an article in an American woman's magazine about scanty panties, he said women who thought about scanty panties never had a comfortable fire burning in the fire-place, or a baby in the house, or a dog or cat or a parrot. . . .

Or a canary, I said.

Or a canary, went on Basil, and he said that this was the end of the moral order.

69

Basil said, if you want to see how cruelly the English can behave you should see them in Kenya and....

Yes, I said hurriedly, it is better for the native population if it is a Crown Colony. If it is a Crown Colony, I said, there is always a fight going on between Whitehall and the planters, which gives the native population the chance to play the one off against the other (and this, I said in an aside to Lopez, is a chance of which they avail themselves). Why, Basil, I said, there is always this fight going on between the planters and the home government, for the planters must get profits, they have sunk their gratuities, they must get money, and so they beat the native employee who is black-faced and unco-operative; the Colonial Secretary of course beats the planters, he has to think of policy, not profits.

And if, said Basil, the poor devil of a native can bring his case to court and the judge rules in his favour then the planters will duck the judge, or if there isn't a pond, they will dip him down the well. And in South Africa, he said, the Boers are the worst of all in their treatment of the black population.

There is nowhere to look, I said, and barely stifled a snigger at the look of satisfaction which came over Basil's face as I said these words. There is something about Basil in his Jeremiac world surveys that turns every woman into a David's wife. But if one laughs in one's heart, one's face preserves a well-bred gloom. For is not this required of one when this David dances before the Ark of Reform, is not this sad face the necessary modicum of good manners? Ahem.

Profits are the devil, I said. In England the wage is the whip, but it is laid on more lightly. I sighed: There is no-where to look. At least, I said, at the moment it is not very good. But there is the possibility we may be coming out, we may just be having our noses out of it, the way we arrange things at present is not the faith once for all delivered to the saints. We might think of something else.

I began to recite them a poem I had just written:

Man is coming out of the mountains
But his tail is caught in the pass,
Why does he not free himself,
Is he not an ass?

Do not be impatient with him,
He is bowed by sorrow and fret,
He is not out of the mountains,
He is not half out yet.

Look at his sorrowful eyes,
His torn cheeks, his brow,
He lies with his head in the dust,
Is there no one to help him now?

No, there is no one to help him,
Let him get on with it,
Cry the ancient enemies of Man
As they cough and spit.

The enemies of Man are like trees,
They stand with the sun in their branches,
Is there no one to help my creature
Where he languishes?

Oh the delicate creature,
He lies with his head in the rubble,
Pray that the moment pass,
And the trouble.

Look he moves—that is more than a prayer,
But he is so slow,
Will he come out of the mountains?
It is touch and go.

Tom stopped reading *The Fairchild Family*, put it in his pocket and walked over to the piano. He began to play a piece out of Beethoven's Funeral Sonata, but very soon he forgot what came next and gave it up.

So long, Celia, he said, so long Lopez, come along Basil.

Basil and Tom went off together, they were going to speak at a meeting.

Lopez said, Vera Hennessey has been, she is coming back, you must wait.

I'll ring up home, I said, because I think my sister Pearl is expected. I say, Lopez, I haven't seen Vera for ages, I didn't know you saw anything of her now. I say Lopez, Clem was going on terribly about Vera the other day, what an ugly devil he is, oh, really, Lopez, he was very spiteful, oh, what a spiteful fellow your brother is.

I suppose he was doing it for Tiny's benefit, said Lopez, no doubt Tiny was also with you.

Oh yes, Lopez, he was, we were all having a nice walk.

Vera crops up you know, she's rather sweet really, but she's a pathological masochist. . . .

What?

Oh yes she is, Basil said she was a pathological masochist.

What on earth does Basil know about it?

Everybody knows that Hennessey treated Vera vilely and that she drew him on. Oh I don't think she really enjoyed it, she just couldn't help herself. He is really violent you know.

Is that what a pathological masochist is? I say, Lopez, wasn't it then—grounds for divorce?

Yes, but she never will, I tell you she cannot help it, she doesn't enjoy it but she has to have it, it goes on and on.

How awful. I say, Lopez, Clem said she was *soumise et peureuse* in manner but something quite different in reality, he hinted that she gave Hennessey a bad time of it, oh gave more than as good as she got.

Don't you believe a word Clem says about that, especially in front of Tiny, he only does it to annoy because he thinks it teases, you know? Ah well, said Lopez, that particular abode of bliss the Hennessey household has now been very thoroughly broken up by the war, so the problem doesn't press, and may very well never press again. Hennessey is now in Malaya. Vera, true to her pathology (you'll see) has joined the WAAFS and won't be out for years. You'll wait?

Rather.

VII

I RANG up home and found my sister had arrived, so I said I must get back to dinner. When Vera came in she looked sweet and desperate. She was on forty-eight hours' leave from the WAAFS. She had put on all her beautiful civilian clothes. She said, Celia, do you like this piece of nonsense? This was her hat which was wonderful.

It is wonderful, Vera, I said, you look wonderful in it.

She told us how terrible it is in the WAAFS. The officers say, Hennessey, I am getting a bit tired of your complaints. She had complained about the food, for there was a war on between the cooks and Admin. and the girls she said were weak for lack of food.

There is no privacy at all, said Vera, and in the end if you are alone you feel distraught, so nervous, you cannot be alone in the end. You have to get your zinc bath and fill it and have your bath and hope that you don't get crabs or syphilis, and there are twenty baths for four hundred girls. The girls are broken, in the end they are broken.

She put her uniform on, I cleaned the buttons for her and Lopez cleaned her shoes. She had to catch the midnight train back to Crewe.

We made her show us how the officers spoke and how it was like when you saw an officer, or got crimed, or asked for compassionate leave.

We acted the officers and then we acted the rankers.

74

Vera said in her tired soft voice: So many girls have committed suicide.

Now at this I suddenly thought, Vera is a tragedienne, she is this, she is very small, much smaller than I am, and she has large dark eyes and this pale desperate look, she is very pretty. She says the girls all say f—, b—, b— my pants, b— f— all the time.

I said: What do they say when they want to say something to make it stand out?

Oh, I don't know, said Vera dreamily.

I said: It is like 'I'll bloody him a bloody fix, I'll bloody burn his bloody ricks'.

What is that? said Lopez.

I came rushing home to see my sister. My sister Pearl said she thought Vera was not absolutely dead right about the WAAFS because she had seen so many of them about Redesdale and they looked happy and that is a thing you do not look if you are both unhappy and broken, as Vera said, because you have not the good morale to look anything but what you are. And Pearl said the girls did not walk looking broken to pieces. So what is the truth of it?

What do the girls make of you, Vera, I said, do they think you are a girl of good family?

I get on with them, said Vera, I think they like me.

And the officers?

They look rather uneasily.

Pearl is so happy at her school now, she has suddenly this warm feeling for everybody, and for her staff-mates, it was not like this quite recently, but now it is. The headmistress

75

says that she is bringing a breath of fresh air and something besides gossip but that the girls are rather frightened of her.

So Pearl tells us that when they were all leaving and the headmistress was there, all the girls ran up crying, Miss Phoze, may I sit beside you, may I sit on your side of the bus? So there is now this warm feeling of shoals safe passed.

I woke at two o'clock this morning because I thought I heard my Aunt cry out, when I went into her bedroom she said she had not cried out but that it was the dog next door and also that five tiles had fallen off the roof in the high wind that was blowing, she had not been to sleep.

I'll get you some tea, Auntie.

Pearl woke up too and came with me.

When we took the tea in to our Aunt she sat straight up in her bed and began telling us about the late vicar of the parish, the vicar who governed our childhood with his loving absentminded ways, whom we dearly loved. This vicar—the Rev. Humphrey d'Aurevilly Cole—had been for many years in love with the organist, a lady of high stomach. There was some trouble between this lady and Humphrey's sister, and the lady said that never would she cross the vicarage doorstep until the sister departed. So in the end the sister died and Humphrey married the organist, and the London papers had a paragraph about it, 'Vicar Marries Organist After Twenty Years' (for twenty years it was).

So we all had a warm and friendly talk about Humphrey, while some more tiles fell off the roof and the June wind roared, and how truly kind he was, and simple, in a way that was often making trouble for him and getting him misunderstood. He was a suffering patient man, a true Christian and a true scholar.

And as we sat talking, I remembered the loving church memories of our childhood, and I remembered Miss Delabole, who used to sit in her bedroom, that was the only room she had, because she had come down in the world, and she was now teaching German, and she was so poor that she could only have a gas ring burning in her room; it was bitter cold, and that was how it was.

I used to sit close beside her to have my German lesson from the Otto-Sauer Grammar, and I used to look at her. She always wore her hat and gloves, her overcoat and her feather boa, sitting indoors, crouching there in front of her gas-ring, with only the one blue gas flame burning for warmth. *Ach, wie furchtbar, so alt zu sein, ach, diese Tränensäcke, als wenn sie viel geweint hätte.*

Sometimes she would forget the German lessons and tell me how it was when she lived in her father's vicarage at Sefton, near Puckley, and how, though the village people went to Puckley every Saturday for market day, they never went so far as the Puckley Junction railway station and had never seen a train. So one day the Vicar took the choirboys to London to go to the Science Museum for a treat, and when they came back it was getting so late, the village people were walking up and down the street and crying: Should they never see their children again, for surely something had happened to them?

But here at last down the village street comes the long thin vicar running swiftly, with his long coat flying out behind him. 'It is all right,' he said, 'we were shunted to Luton by mistake, the children are coming.' So then the children came, and it was a quarter to twelve at night.

My father, said Miss Delabole, was a very earnest man, he loved the church; we girls used to sit and make the surplices for the choir, because there was no money to buy any, we made them all, but the people did not like the surplices. It was then that the farmer's wife left the church; she said it was Popery.

In those days, said Miss Delabole, the church of England slept, the bishops were so indifferent and so casual; well, she said, I remember at the confirmation service the bishop would just play his hands down the row of little girls, and say the words not for each little girl separately, but making once do for the whole front row, and so on to the second row, and the third; and when the Dean of Westminster went into the Abbey on Christmas morning he saw only seven people were there, so he said: 'Not enough,' and went home.

The Church slept then, you cannot imagine it.

So long, I said, to Auntie and my sister, and I strolled back to my room and I got into bed, still thinking of Miss Delabole and the Church of England, with an: 'Ah how can a child understand,' and a 'Now, Patsy (for so I was then called), get on with your reading, *Es war einmal ein Königssohn . . . und so weiter*'.

For a long time I lay wakeful, turning my head upon the pillow, and still could not sleep, and still the stone hot water bottle leaped heavily upon me.

So now that I knew I could not sleep (for the stone hot water bottle and the uncomfortable pillow), I turned towards the window and looked out of the window at our tree waving black against the night sky. Since I was a child we have been in this house and in this quiet faubourg where the air blows so fresh through the broken windowpanes. It is high up on the north London hills. At the top of our hill they say with pride that we are the highest point between where we are and the Ural Mountains.

Our tree waves black against the sky to-night, the wind is rising. The tree blows about and casts black shadows in our yard. Our tree, our yard, how agreeable is the possessive feeling, our stove has gone to be mended, our pipe is burst, our dishcloth has washed down the drain, our kettle empties as it boils, our teapot does not pour. Often I hear my aunt scolding the inanimate things, 'stupid, why must you do that?'

By the dustbin in the corner of our yard it is as black as ink. Once we had a rat, he used to sit and grind his teeth; if you looked out of the window there he was in the middle of the yard as large as a dog. He had a hole by the dustbin. When the dustmen came they saw our rat and heaved a brick at him. 'That's done him,' they cried. That indeed had, he was dead, they had done him in.

My aunt was not at all pleased when I told her at breakfast that the dustmen had killed our rat. But I remember the occasion passed off all right, for at that time my aunt was full of the famous quarrel that was going on between the two parish ladies who had fallen out while tending the graves of their husbands who lay side by side in the Scapeland cemetery. Mrs. Jale was a real grievous widow, with a drip at the end of her nose, she had led her husband a sorry life, but now he was dead she mourned him with a vengeance. Mrs. Jelliband, the other lady, had a warm wit and bright affections. She, too, mourned her dear one, who had been her dear one all her life, she mourned him truly, but the Jale one said that she was heartless, for once she had heard her say: 'Oh for an afternoon off. Oh for a few minutes to call my own.' So Mrs. Jale said to Mrs. Jelliband: 'Now you have your wish, now you have more than a few minutes to yourself, now you have more than an afternoon off.'

Oh, the wicked cruel woman, said my Aunt, telling the story.

Mrs. Jelliband never spoke to Mrs. Jale again. 'If,' she said, 'I should meet her now in the cemetery, I do not know that I could keep my fingers to myself.'

I fell asleep and dreamt that I walked into the bathroom and found one of my sister's shoes half afloat in shallow water. Who has left the tap running? I cried out and woke myself.

To-day is the last day before the holiday. I walk out early into the early morning sunshine. I walk out to do the early morning shopping before I go to the Ministry.

When I come back with my shopping basket full of what I have been fetching, Kathie is at our gate with her bicycle.

Kathie is a girl in this suburb who brings me lettuces and onions from her allotment.

On, Kathie, what lovely lettuces—and onions.

I am so glad to have caught you before you leave for your Ministry.

Well, I say, I am going late to-day because to-night I am working on night shift.

Ah. When does your leave start, Celia?

Why to-morrow, Kathie, I leave early to-morrow morning.

You are going to Lincolnshire to stay with your Uncle Heber?

Why, yes.

Your Aunt does not see her brother very often now, does she?

Who is this coming down the road, Kathie, with a bowler hat on his head and a shovel in his hand?

It is old Mr. Entwhistle on his way to the allotment.

No, my Aunt does not see very much of her brother.

Last year she called for afternoon tea with Pearl, who was passing in her car on the way to Hull.

She is not going again this year?

No, she does not like to leave this house for very long. Now the war is over my Aunt feels that the house must not be left; during the war it has stood so much so now it must not be left.

Will your cousin be there?

Yes, I think he will be there.

Your cousin Casmilus?

My cousin Casmilus. My cousin Tom will not see his father. He has not seen his father now since he first left home.

Casmilus was seconded to Intelligence, was he not?

Yes, that is right Kathie.

I admire Kathie, this Kathie is a girl who loves her mother and hates her papa, she is a cantankerous inquisitorial devil, but staunch and true, with a mind made up once and for all upon all knotty problems.

Kathie is doing voluntary work in connection with the After-Care Centre. She does not like the way some of those young girls go on.

The way those girls go on, she says.

Oh yes, isn't it awful?

Isn't what awful? says Kathie.

Oh, I say quickly, the way those young girls go on.

I'm on leave too next week, said Kathie, I am going to stay with Mabel. We may be able to see something of each other.

(Mabel lives ten miles from Uncle Heber's.)

Oh yes, I say, isn't it awful.

Isn't what awful?

What? Oh, the way those young girls go on, what did you think, Kathie?

I take my luggage up to the Ministry with me. It is night now and my night-shift has begun, it is now the half-hour break period. I am sitting on a sandbag in the shadow of the west tower of the Ministry. I am feeling rather excited because I am waiting for Caz to come. The full moon is now aloft, it is shining in a calm night sky, there is that sense of a great depth one might fall off into. It is a fine melancholy scene in the grand manner. How melancholy and grand the great tower stands up. In a few hours from now my holiday will begin.

VIII

A T TWO A.M. my cousin Caz comes round the corner. He whistles softly.

Caz, I say, over here.

He comes over.

All set for the eight o'clock train, he says, he sits down beside me on the sandbag and sighs happily, I've got the tickets and a locked carriage.

He pulls me up and gives me a quick hug, O.K. for priority. I'll see you at the barrier.

He comes back and says, Tiny is coming. I couldn't help it, Celia, you know what Heber feels about it, he insisted.

I begin to toss and fret. Oh heaven's a locked carriage all the way to Staunton-le-Hodge with Tiny and Caz, oh heavens, that is something.

As soon as the train has pulled out of the station Caz pulls me down on to his knees. He puts his arm round me, oh heavens, this is comfortable.

How lovely to see you, Tiny. Why are we having Tiny? I say to Caz.

Uncle Heber thinks Tiny is a likely lad.

Tiny looks pleased.

Tiny, darling, you do look pleased. Isn't it wonderful that we have our leave together?

Oh yes, says Tiny, isn't it wonderful?

I can't think how they can spare Tiny, can you, Caz?

No, I can't think that.

I tell Caz about Tom, the night in the studio.

How awful I must have looked, lying on my scarlet coat. Afterwards I put my Burberry on.

You don't mean to say, said Tiny, that you put that awful Burberry on top of your scarlet coat?

Oh yes I did, I said. The scarlet coat was too fine, it was much too fine. But the mackintosh hid it all, it was the right coat to wear. *Ça, c'était robe de style Hobo.* I turned my face against my cousin's shoulder.

Celia, how you do go on, he said.

Well, one does go on you know.

When was all this?

It was last week.

Oh, well, I suppose you may go on a little bit.

Oh, thank you, Tiny, what a comfort you are. Oh, I'm so glad we have Tiny with us. Oh, Uncle Heber will be so glad.

Did our cousin Tom say anything? said Caz.

Not one word.

He always was a morbid chap, said Tiny, I remember him at school.

Oh, Tiny, what a memory you have.

I should imagine him talking all the time about the revolution.

Oh, that is not right, Tiny, he would not talk about the revolution.

Or about the deviationist opinions of Prodko.

No, no, that is not right.

Or about fishing, said Caz.

That is more like it.

Or about the Petainismus of the younger poets.

84

Yes, that is quite right.

It is rather like that Cochran review sketch, you know; the girl and the boy are twisting and turning upon the promenade bench.

Oh, yes, I remember the twisting and turning.

And all the time the girl is saying how the landlady did not give her a second helping of semolina pudding, and how the steak and kidney pie was chilled.

Oh, yes, that is how it was, it was chilled.

He always was a morbid chap, said Tiny, looking out of the window. By Jove, he said, there's a crested hawk.

No, not a crested hawk, I say, sitting up to look. Oh, Tiny, that is just like Tom. And suddenly I love Tom and forget him.

How is Uncle Heber, Caz?

Oh, so so, madder than ever, your know, you'll see. How is Aunt?

Oh, she is wonderful, well, she has this new dress with poppies all over it, it is like Carter's Tested Seeds. It is called, Every One Came Up.

I now went to lie down on the seat opposite and I slept right through till lunchtime. Tiny had brought a lunch basket, he had thought of everything, or somebody had. We had cress and spam sandwiches, ginger biscuits, a large whale-oil cake from Benthun's, a tea kettle and some tea in mesh bags. I gave Tiny the mesh bags. A rich mean relation in Seattle, State of Washington, had sent them to Auntie for a Christmas present instead of candies.

I said: Did you know Tengal was at Stoneyhurst?

I saw him for a minute or two at Lopez's party the other evening, began Tiny, conversationally.

Listen. Tengal was a very pious boy and when he was at Stoneyhurst he set such a pace in piety and religious

85

observation it was an embarrassment to the priests, he knew all about this and that, and serving mass, and singing seconds in the choir, and he said it was very beautiful and very, very rich in emotion, and that it was a good thing because it was better than playing it off at football and cricket. He said that once every year they had a Retreat, and the boys were so worked upon by the sermons and the silence, and then the sermons again, and thinking about the Passion, they used to cry, they used to kneel there crying. And then the priest would say: 'Eternity, eternity, eternity, and in hell not one moment is free from pain, for do not suppose that the senses are dulled, as by the mercy of Our Lady they are dulled for us who are in pain in the earthly body. But in hell the senses are eternally revived to receive an eternal pain that is eternally as a fresh pain freshly received, except that the weakness and the memory of past pain, that is so actual a part of pain, is there too, so that the quivering nerves receive it as a fresh pain, but the mind knows it as familiar, acute, and eternally endurable by reason of the vigour that is poured into the nerves and bones and arteries of the damned.'

I sighed, I said: It is like the Italian story I read, it was called *Una Settimana in Paradiso*, it was about these little girls who were to have a Retreat before making their first communion, they were poor children and could not have afforded a Retreat, but the Pope paid for them. The nuns said, '*Paga il Papa.*' And the joy and the terror of the Passion was played upon them, and they were pierced with joy and terror, and they brushed their hair and had pale faces and burning eyes, and they prayed to the Virgin in ecstasy, they were quite split up and open, and they remembered the Pope paid, and they cried in simplicity and gratitude, '*Paga il Papa.*' This was a simple story I forget who it was by.

You know, Casmilus and Tiny, I tell you these things,

I remember them, but I have no great knowledge of the foreign languages (I sigh), I have a superficial mind and but a smattering. So that for instance although I have read a great many simple stories in the foreign languages, I have not read the classics, because my acquaintance with the language is not sufficient, it is, you understand, not quite strong enough for the classics. (I sigh again.)

Tiny has now dozed off; I turn to Caz.

So that I did not read Dante, you will understand that is difficult, but I can remember the lines that I have heard said, I whisper in my cousin's ear, '*Galeotto fu il libro e chi lo scrisse, e quel giorno piu non vi leggemmo avanti*'.

Not quite that, said Caz.

Oh, well (I hurry on), and I did not read *I Promessi Sposi*. And in German I did not read *Dichtung und Wahrheit* or *Die Leute von Seldwyla* or *Die Bernstein Hexe*.

Caz now has his left arm round me, he begins to stroke and pat.

But, Caz, that last one I did read *in*, and I remember this amber witch-girl was going to be burnt, and her parents were so sad, for it was a frame-up. No witch was this girl. So they came to the place where their girl lay in prison, and what could they bring her for a present but tears and sorrow and parting? So what could they bring her? They brought her flax, that she might bind it round her body and so burn more quickly. I began to cry out and wring my hands. Ah, ah, ah. What was that for a present to bring their darling girl? They had better brought her a knife to cut her throat, or a poison flask. But they were these Germans, this lamentable people, that are so hysterical and docile and unfree, so they could not be so sturdy and free to take the sturdy and free way out, and so die to cheat the hangman. Oh, no, for the Germans, with their shining mad eyes, hold fast to pain and take pride in it. *Je grösser der Schmerz, desto besser das Kind*. Ah, ah, ah. Oh, would to God the Romans had ploughed them utterly up, oh, would to God that Europe might be quit of them for ever. Oh, would to God the German women might die, what matter how many manic-depressives fell on the Eastern Front, while the women still live and breed?

Always there is this war between Germany and England: Oh, how the English do not understand. In the beginning of the war I went to a meeting in the House of Commons with a German refugee professor. England, he said, is biological. This meeting was held by the Cambridge Peace Aims group, and in the Chair was Sir Richard Acland, flanked by three undergraduates, looking pretty serious. So everybody was thinking what to do with Germany after the war. And not for one moment did anybody think that we might lose this war, though there we were, unprepared and un-military, at war with the great hysterical military patient-preparing nation that for ten years had ruled for war.

Caz had stood up and pushed me backwards, and was lying on top of me, and had taken my head in his hands, and was looking at me in a casual way.

Listen, Caz, *Achtung!* Please pay attention. Freud said that Germany had the greatest death-wish in the world of any nation. And when I came out of this meeting, I tucked my arm into the arm of the German professor who was beginning to cry for all the nonsense that had been spoken at the meeting, and for the way the English people did not understand about Germany. And silently the tears fell down, he did not sob. So I thought the common people were right, they were saying: Now Germany has asked for it, now she has asked for it, now she will get it. And

I made a jingo poem, Caz, and I said: For every blow they inflict on Jewry, And other victims of their fury, They ask for death on bended knee, And we will give them death and we Will give them death to three times three. And then, Caz, we went to a coffee bar in the House of Commons and had some terrible coffee and sandwiches. And we looked out of the windows of the House of Commons on to the blank plains of war. And the professor said: England is certainly biological, but oh, if she would only come to it more quickly, and (he said) if I may add, in the end with less impetus, for there will be very little left when she has finished.

There was silence now in our railway carriage, but there must not be silence. I looked up into my cousin's face that was so close to mine, no there must not be silence.

His eyes were no longer looking at me, they were turned to the window with an abstracted expression, he lay close and heavy on top of me, looking out of the window but not looking, not looking at all anywhere. Caz, I cried, Caz.

When I was staying in India when I was a child, when I was staying with Uncle Edmund and Aunt Eva, when my father brought me out to stay with them, I used to play with my cousin Caz, and I used to go playing with him and with the dear fellow Raji, whom we then first met, playing as children in the Indian hot sunshine.

And I used to go playing with my cousin down by the river, and one day we were going along, and suddenly across a narrow stretch of creek in the river bank on the other side, we saw a young panther that had made a kill, that was lying on top of his kill, that was about to tear the heart out of it. Well, for some slight noise, or for the smell of us coming up the wind, the panther suddenly raises his head and looks across at my cousin and me; but then his glance slips sideways, and still he looks intently, but looks at nothing, and in a minute he turns to his kill again and will tear the heart out of it; this minute was a time-pause, a break, now he turns to his kill. So this is the abstracted time-pause moment that sits now in my cousin's eyes, this is the look he now has.

Oh, my sly father, the sly foxy creature; they say that he was sweet on Aunt Eva, very warm and close he was, very coaxing. Caz said it was an old story. My father was a fox.

Caz, I cry, Caz. How long will the post-war last, Caz, shall we win the post-war, how does it go?

So so, said Caz, getting up with a smile. He sits down in the corner and gives Tiny a jog with his feet as he swings them up on to the seat. So so, we rub along, another ten years or so will see us over the worst. We are vacillating lazy and slow, but we have never in all our history for one moment entertained the idea that it might be a good thing to lose a fight. We are not a sophistical people and are saved the dangers that run with sophism; and our education has not yet succeeded in taking away from us the weapons of our strength—insularity, pride, xenophobia and good humour.

When we get to the station our darling Uncle Heber is there. I put my arms round his neck and kiss him. He is old and grey, in a long green-black coat, it is a dust coat, it is long like a dressing-gown.

Oh, darling Uncle Heber, I say, at last we are here.

The train is quite punctual, Celia, quite upon time. How do you do, Tiny? Ah, Casmilus.

When we arrived at the rectory (Uncle drove us out in the dog-cart and if one of us had to get out going uphill to save the pony Caramel, that one was Tiny), we had some cold lamb, some chopped cold cabbage, some home-made sour milk cheese, and some beastly cocoa.

There are some spring onions in the cupboard, if any person cares for such things, said my Uncle in a low faint voice.

I had had enough of company by now, so I went upstairs early to my old-fashioned bedroom. This was a large low room with bow windows, there was a smaller room opening out of it which was a dressing room, there was a large tin hip bath on the floor.

My uncle's old maid Tuffie was in this room, spreading a blanket under the bath. There was a large jug of boiling water on the floor beside the bath. I kissed Tuffie and looked out of the window at the twilight dark sky. It was getting late.

You'll want another jug, said Tuffie.

I'll carry it up, Tuffie.

I went down to the kitchen with her to fetch the water, we drew it off the boiling copper.

Oh, how lovely it smells, Tuffie, I said, opening the kitchen door to smell the late evening smell of the kitchen garden.

I made two more journeys to refill the jugs with cold water, and Tuffie gave me a large pre-war tablet of soap. Now I was ready, the old cold sponge was there that I remembered from my many visits, the soap, and enough cold water. That is a thing that must not be forgotten when you are having a boiling water hip bath, if you forget you have to dress again and wait for the boiling water to cool.

I mixed the water to the right heat and got into my bath, the water slopped over on to the blanket as I sat down cross-legged with my back up against the chair-back end of the bath. The water was soft as silk.

I dried myself quickly and got into bed. I could look through the window from where I lay, the sky was now the colour of full night.

I thought, I am a middle-class girl, conditioned by middle-class thoughts, when I think of England, my dear country, I think with pride, aggression and complacency. I tie up my own pride and advantage with England's, I have no integrity, no honesty, no generous idea of a better way of life than that way which gives cream to England. But where can one get this idea of a new world, and how can one believe it? The people are like me, they are awful; they are not like me, they are awful. I saw the good stupid faces before I left London, crowding with seven children the streets and the shops, you could not move in Oxford Street for the people agape with seven children. How can people be different, eh? People say people were heroic in the raids. They were certainly good humoured and plucky and uncomplaining, but is it heroism to endure the unavoidable? Is not heroism rather to seek an end through danger? There was no end thought of or sought.

I now get out of bed to go and hang out of the window to look at the moon that is shining bright and mellow; the full moon is coming up over the fields.

How bright the moon shines, how mellow, how calm, and how with the yellow mild light the memories and the happiness run backwards to my heart, the blood turns, it is warm and mellow, the blood flows back to the heart.

In India we children never went to bed when we should; we went to bed but we got up again, we loved to run out again, in our nightclothes, out to the balcony that hung from our window, the lofty flying balcony with its delicate wrought iron balustrade. The fine tracery was black as ink against the Indian full moon, that was fuller and nearer than

92

this English moon, more powerful, less mild, rather disturbing, the Indian full moon.

It was in India that we first met the dear fellow Raji, as a child, as children; our black playfellow, our Raji. But now when Caz meets Raji in London, he laughs, he says: Eh, Raji, you are going round the parties, eh, you would rather be a party-pet in London than a martyr to your opinions in Bangalore, eh, Raji? And so there is not a friendly feeling between them.

Next week my cousin will be in Delhi, he is flying back to India, he is posted to Delhi.

In the moonlight Lincolnshire garden in the dark shadows below the cedar tree it is like India, I have the feeling it is India before me and not England; it is warmer, it grows warm and close, the night has a wild smell, a smell of dung, of sour smoke, of a magnolia, of a heavy scent, of a scent you would say if you had it in a bottle: It is a cheap scent, it is something from the market stall, from the open market stalls in Cambridge, eh, where I once bought such a bottleful. 'It is the sort of thing,' the Cambridge don said, 'that my hairdresser presses me to buy.'

Raji was beaten for his opinions when he was agitating in India; he was slung from side to side of the prison yard by the Indian policemen.

My cousin Caz was once beaten by some Jewish Zionist terrorists, he was taken off and beaten, and afterwards they gave him some propaganda books to read, and they were nervous and they giggled, but my cousin was wrapped away in bitter anger, he would not read. My cousin said that they wished most of all that he would look at them, speak to them; say that somehow, in some way he understood, that he who was in the top prestige group of all, a British officer, in uniform, with the long centuries of

93

government behind him, must now be beaten by the land-less and lowest, must be beaten and must understand. And knowing this, and understanding all too well, even so Caz would not look at them, would not speak, would not give them one look. He blamed himself to me; but it was, he said, the anger that ran high, and ran between them. I could have afforded to speak to them, he said. You know, Celia, I was wrapping myself in my anger, and he sighed, I am often lost, too, he said, we know what we ought to do, he said, and we wrap ourselves against it, in anger, in pomposity, in some justice, anything, to be wrapped away from what we ought to do.

We are right to quit India. So long as England rules India so long will the scent of the cheap bottle of scent on the Cambridge stall be the scent of India. It is good for nothing and nobody.

In the days before the war a free India was a fine free song for the fine free hearts of America, and a fine sure twist for the old Lion's tail. It is indeed instructive to see how the tune has now changed and how it is likely to change into something quite different in the near future. They're a bit edgy now about Congress, Congress don't look so good. Their hearts go out to England now, it certainly is tough for England having those Congress chaps on her tail. For if England quits India now, what about that base against their arch enemy old J. Stalin, and what about India's lovely markets, eh? what about them, a fellow has to think realisti-cally. How can they work up the consumer mind in India's millions with no benevolent British Government in the saddle? Eh, that will be difficult. The British may be slow and snooty, but they're fundamentally sound, they don't go monkeying with markets, they can be relied upon for a kind of reverent attitude to markets. On the other hand—

and here the other tune starts up—America might back the English out and come in after them, arriving nicely in time to shove the U.S.S.R. off the northern approaches and so grab the markets for themselves. So she'll keep her Pearl Bucks and Norah Walns on tap—she may want 'em yet.

I was once going to a meeting in London where Raji was speaking, he was reading a paper on the English novelists that write about India, and I was thinking it would be nice if it was something about *In Old Madras*, a book I read when I was a young child, it was about a man that got his nose cut off in the Mutiny and so lived for ever after with a black patch stuck on his face; this book was running very strong and vivid, with the atmosphere and the black faces. But no .... Of course, first of all our Raji had to be introduced by the lady that was in the Chair. So this lady spoke at great length about all the people she had known and loved in India, and about the children she had reared, and their lovely Ayah, their dog and their washerman.

Everybody in this room that I could see as I glanced casual-like around me, seemed to be an Anglo-Indian of previous importance, except for a few Indians who looked scornful and angry.

There was now some applause for the lady, and then silence for Raji to begin his talk. He spoke quickly and rather softly; at the back of the room nobody could hear a word, but the English were too polite to say so. An Indian, however, with a spiteful look, handed up a note to say: Louder and slower.

Of course, as I had a friendly familiar feeling for old Raji, I could not listen closely to his talk.

So after Raji had finished speaking, an Englishman got up and made a good speech and he said that after living forty-one years in India he would still hardly presume to write a word about India. Not so, he said, those who came on a short visit. He said that *The Rains Came* was the best novel about the Middle West he had ever read.

The English in the room now laughed and applauded, so I saw that for all their sleepy look they were well awake. A young violent English person now got up to say that no easy feeling of equality between intellectual Indians and English people was possible in India so long as this evil thing (the British Raj) was still in existence. Affection there might be, of a feudal variety, between the governing English and the simple people of India, but for the intellectual Indians, no.

This remark caused great offence among the English, and a man sitting next to me, with a Roman face and heavy cheek jowls, got slowly to his feet and said, 'I disagree', and sat down.

There were several Roman-faced English judge-like people sitting together in the back row. For the present they neither spoke nor clapped. Later they might come to the summing up and the advising of the jury, but not here and not to-day.

An elderly whitehaired man of magnificent appearance now rose to address the meeting. He had the governing appearance; he had, in the quieter generations, governed Bengal. Bengal, he said, had been the Cinderella of the provinces, but he had drained, and built, and irrigated, and now she was the Queen of all the provinces. As he spoke the hot winds blew and the jungle grass parted and the swamps swung heavy upon primeval silt. And in the fierce summers the ladies moved up to the hills, and the English men stayed behind and, growing angrier, worked and raged and maddened.

We shall never budge, I thought, shift we may, on our own terms, but budge, never.

And I thought again of Rome, that was taken captive, that had captured the world. And I thought: Happier the ancient world, with Rome for an adversary, the Rome that could be broken and done with; but the British are like water that shifts to its own course.

This was a happy occasion for the ageing Governor, for now he was back in India again, in the Queen of the provinces. He began to speak with great love of the country, and of his years of fruitful work, and of his dog, that was called Lumpton. This was a fine animal that had hunted the tiger and the lion and the gazelle and the snakes. The dog, he said, was a creature of great dignity and coursed swiftly.

Lopez, who was with me at this meeting, dismissed the speaker abruptly: He is a blimp. But the violent young man, who had spoken of the intellectual Indians, said: 'That is their answer.' So the meeting was now over, but when I was going out I hooked my arm into dear Raji's, with my other arm round Lopez, and I said: I also was a crowned child in a subject land, I also was in India. So we came away, and it was over.

In Raji's own book that he wrote, that is so true about India, and so much the book that English people ought to read, and is so much the book that so many of them do not want to read, why in this book Raji says that the English are practically invisible in India, by reason of the anger and the pride, and that all the cruelty there is, and the beastliness, is done by avaricious middlemen and Indian paid subordinates, and by the rich Muslim trading families, like the great mill-owning rich families of Bombay. And he says that one of the most oppressive things the English have brought to India is that sense of secret opulence in a land of poverty, and this opulence shows itself in close-curtained bungalows with plain outsides, and the luxury going on within in a secret way, not sin, mind you, which anyone could understand, but just plain comfort, unindictable, untouchable, invisible and foreign.

I begin to have a certain memory now of the time when I was in India. One day when I was with my cousin Caz, I stood parting the swinging bead curtain to come through with him and out into the compound beyond the sitting-room open long windows. And there in the sitting-room, on the sofa, was my Aunt Eva, Caz's mama, and there beside her knelt my father, and he was speaking to her and crying. He was sobbing. Caz led me off, they did not see us. But we heard what my father said; he said: 'To hell with Edmund.'

This was in the hot weather, when my Uncle Edmund used to take us to stay at a small place beside the sea, where we stayed in a palace that was very ramshackle that a prince had lent him. My Uncle Edmund was deeply read in Indian lore and art, and this prince was a firm friend of his.

I remember this day very well, because later we picked up our friend Raji, who lived close by, and we all went to bathe in the river, where we were allowed to bathe at a special place.

As we came out from the room where my father knelt beside Aunt Eva, Caz said to me in a cold clear voice: 'It is an old story.' All day he was white-faced and angry, and he was reckless and mad. We were not allowed to walk along the high stone walls that bordered the narrows where the river dipped and flowed swift and deep. But now Caz walked along this wall and dared Raji to follow him and to jump across to the wall opposite that held the river. It was a mad jump, but Caz took off well and brought it off. Raji stood holding my hand and laughing: 'it will be all right,' he said, 'he is mad and only a mad person could make a success of it, so he will make a success of it.' When Caz came back to us and saw Raji still laughing and holding my hand, he flew into a great passion and knocked Raji down and began to pummel his head. Caz, you are mad, I said, stop. And I begin to kick him to make him stop being so mad. Raji stood up and looked at both of us with a quite extraordinary look—very grown-up, sorrowful, gentle, dark and dignified. Then he marched off and left us together. 'Now you are offended, I suppose?' said Caz. Yes, you may suppose I am. But I was thinking of my father and Aunt Eva, and I began to sob and snuffle, as did Caz also. And we lay down together crying bitterly, and it was from here, across the creek, that I looked up when we had been crying for a long time, and I looked up and there was the great panther that I have spoken of, lying close upon his kill, looking across at us, and then looking sideways, intently, away, upon nothing.

My Uncle Edmund had a governing job of some sort, and for the greater part of each year he lived in a fine cool stone house in a jungle district. So there was the tropic jungle all round us, and the great tank in the compound, with the dead toads in it, and some live ones, too, I dare say, and so on. And this place was my chief memory of India, for it was only once in the year and for a short time that we were down by the sea in the Prince's palace, though Raji would come up sometimes and stay with us in the stone house and bring the sea memories to us again.

And I remember there was an ape that went with the house. And we children, that is my cousin and I, used to watch him as he swung, swinging at midnight in the moonlight. Caz and I were rather frightened and disturbed by the midnight jungle and the full moon, and we slept together always for comfort and company, and I remember him now in my arms, and how sweet he was, he was my true friend then, as also he is now.

So India and its fevers links with this cool Lincolnshire, where now we are, where now we are; and both again beneath an uncle's roof.

(This ape that went with the house was called Sinbad, he was already an old animal. The poor ape, the poor beast, you would say, to be so old and so sick, and yet alive, alive-o. Believe me, Reader, that animal was happy in a quiet way, swinging at his own sweet will in the warm southern night and the mellow moonbeam.)

So this is the other side of the question, of the famous old bogey-question of England-in-India, yes, this is the other side of that. And how can we leave India when we have these loving memories, how can we do it?

I was feeling pretty wild by now, with the tears coming running down my face for the thoughts and the memories, and with the clock striking three in the morning, I hung out of the window, looking far out into the dark night. Oh, dark Lincolnshire, how beautiful you are. So with this loving thought in my mind, I get back into my bed and fall asleep.

IX

TUFFIE CAME INTO my room at eight o'clock for a chat. I put on my shirt and shorts and went down and had breakfast with her in the kitchen. We generally had our meals there, it was a large untidy sort of place.

Tuffie said Uncle was melancholy-like. She said that never would he get over Master Tom. (Oh, my poor Heber, how intransigent the mad Tom is. The trouble between them was not in the realm of reason, it was not knowable, it lay down, wrapped in the lowlying mists of madness, no use to think of it.)

Tuffie said it had been raining a lot, and the rain was melancholy-like. But Tuffie was not melancholy, she was a fine London woman from Tufnell Park that got a bit homesick sometimes and liked to hear the London news. I told her that the London children were still playing their war games. There was a little boy that used to ride his tricycle outside our house. He went round and round upon his tricycle and all the time he was shouting: 'Coming in to attack, coming in to attack.' Old Mr. Entwhistle, at the bottom of our street, was wheeling his grandchild home in her go-cart packed out with beer bottles. He was a fond cheerful granddad, and when he stopped to tuck the baby's rug in he saw that her nose was running. 'Wipe your nose, you dirty cat,' he said. She was his favourite grandchild, his dear one.

I did not want to see the others, so I was glad to have my breakfast early. I helped Tuffie wash up, and then I cut myself a piece of cake and went off for the morning across the park towards the lake.

I walked across the lawns and through the oakwoods, which smelled very sweet after the rain, and the sun was now strong and drew up the moisture. It was a truly desolate scene, such as I am partial to. On the surface of the lake lay a white mist where the water drew off. The parkland, sunlit and remote, fell away from the river on the other side, and the grass growing on the gravel paths, and the untidy rhododendron bushes gave the whole thing an air of ramshackle aristocracy. A sarcophagus in the distance pointed the tale of decay and put me in mind of Henry James's heroine, privately bred and fallen on hard times. The whole scene as I surveyed it seemed almost too good to be true, it was a real collector's piece. But how refreshing in certain moods are things in decay, and in the same mood how horrible when in the course of nature decay passes to change and life renews itself in brassy forms.

But now the earth's moisture, drawn in spirals round my knees, struck upward to my heart, and I was oppressed by such a sense of melancholy sweet sadness, of a tragedy of huge dimension but uncertain outline, of wrongs forgotten whose pain alone remains, that I cried out in fear and threw myself upon the ground. There is not one thing in life, I cried, to make it bearable.

I decided to go for a swim. I walked round the lake and above the lake where the river ran into it I found an old tree with its branches bent low upon the water. I took off my clothes, and crawling along a branch dropped into deep water. I swam straight out and turned on my back to let the current carry me down into the lake. Oh, God, I thought, we are not innocent, yet innocence is what one would wish for. The water was as cold as ice. I had a sleepy feeling that I was floating away from the Ministry, and the London parties, and Lopez, and the Indian problems, and going to have a fine long sleep and no dreams.

My cousin got me out. He had been riding in the park, having saddled the old horse Noble and stirred him to a canter. He saw me floating past. He looked furious, and started rubbing my wrists and ankles, and pouring brandy down my throat. I lay for a long time on some moss, in the full sun, with my eyes shut.

It is not that life is so awful, but that I am, there is no end to the pain and fear, and to the general shiftiness of my character, I said, as it were to God, but actually to Caz. He had retrieved my clothes and I was dressed, he was holding my hand.

This is the best place on earth for me, I said, I should not wish to leave it.

When Caz plunged into the lake to get me out, he was streaming beside me, laughing and crying out: Death, Death, a thousand smiling faces.

Why, Caz, I said, you are quite mad about death.

How pleasant it is to drift along the swift current of a river, and if at a distance you hear, full fathom falling many more than five, the fall of the river over rocks from a height, does it matter? Drift, drift, go with it, ride the rocks and the hazard, it is a chance—tipped lightly by a wish?

There was no waterfall, I said.

No, but the water is cold, said my cousin, and the currents where it joins the lake are strong and under-surface.

Kathie is staying with Mabel, I said.

By this time he had got me upon Noble and had me on the saddle in front of him. I felt very happy now as we ambled gently through the park together, and I lent back against him as heavily as I could for company.

I love Kathie, said Caz, she is such a strong old crab, always so much herself.

Yes, I said, I love Kathie too. (I laughed to think of Kathie.) I say: She is this purposeful girl, this bitter pill; my word, she is a bitter pill. Oh, Caz, what a grind that poor beast has for her living. She adores M., you know, her employer, but is exasperated by him; she earns very little money, but is staunch, and so honest and decided. She loves her mama, she is a hundred years older than this flighty mama, she is a mother to her mother. She hates her papa with an ugly burning hatred. Old M., her employer, is of course on velvet. There is no work he can pile on her that she does not accept; she has the honour to be the sort of girl no work can floor. A cross-patch, yes; but a floored girl, never. She is a *bonne-a-tout-faire* with a vengeance. She is also a middle-class conform person.

Caz, I said, it is funny how Basil and the chums are still in this violent revolt from the virtues of the middle-classes; it must be a sort of snobism, it has to be that. But perhaps it is only partly that, only a little snobism but chiefly a restless and temperamental dislike of that type of person. If it was not for Basil and Lopez and you and me, and perhaps Tiny, the middle-classes would be unbearable. But also without the middle-classes we should be unbearable. There must be that variety of virtue as of experience. Basil is strong, simple, with a fine writer's mind and the reasonable faith of an intelligent revolutionary. These people see the middle-classes as obstructionist box-dwellers, whose only thought is for themselves and for their families, as if that was not the common thought of the greater part of mankind. The free-blowing revolutionaries, the classless artists, these are the salt of the earth, for they have the power to see a thing while it is yet a long way off. But you cannot make a diet of salt, and it is through the use and practice of the middle-classes that the vision is made actual. I have not found the middle-classes against the new ideas, so much as anxious how they may be applied; but of course I am speaking of the less wealthy sort of middle-class person, such as we have at home.

Caz said that that was the word, anxiety was the burden of their lives, that had many other burdens too; they could not have the gay and lackadaisical carelessness of the poor, who, living from hand to mouth, did indeed take no thought for the morrow; they could not have this, because the set-up of their minds, even more than their incomes, was different; they so badly wanted to establish themselves and their children, and went to great lengths of self-sacrifice and hardship to do this; and if the idea of establishment was itself paltry and ignoble, about that way of life, and the sacrifice, there was something neither paltry nor ignoble, though shadowed and not free, as we should like people to be free.

At the peak of the London and Liverpool and Hull and Southampton and Portsmouth air-raids, you know, I said, there were people watching and assessing, and the upshot of their conclusions was that it was these small middle-class people who were steadiest under fire, who did not panic, who were capable of organizing themselves into small groups, to help the people and cope with the situations.

Now Blind, I said, that poet, and his friends, and that friend Tengal, they are always saying we must break up the middle-class home-block, teach them to have communal interests, to form reading groups, play and health centres. Et cetera. But I really am contemptuous when I hear this, for I live among them, and it is only by a temperamental difference, that is indeed very strong in me, that I have avoided being drawn into these groups; for they have them, I assure you, they have them already. There is the Art Circle, the Shakespeare Reading Society, the Player's Guild (associated with our local theatre), the Library Discussion Group, the Communist Party and the Labour Party, the Liberal Party, and even the Primrose League. Why should Blind suppose he has anything to teach them in the matter of group activities? How can he be so stupid as to imagine that? Eh, that is absurd.

Caz said that this sort of thing would also bore him to tears, and he thought the pleasantness of my life with my Aunt was just that neither of us liked groups, and that both of us liked different things, and that I had this quiet place to come home to, and this beautiful quiet empty house, and the beautiful food that my Aunt cooked for me, and the fondness that my Aunt had for me, that is something even more than the fondness people have for the people they cook food for. And that all the time, if I fell sad, there were the streets and the parks full of these happy but different people.

Oh, how I wished sometimes that Caz might come to visit us in our quiet suburb, but this I did not say, for this was not possible. My Aunt never spoke of Caz, she did not know that I saw him; she did not wish us to associate, because of Aunt Eva.

Oh, I said, often when I am sad I go up to the park and take a deck chair and sit under the oak trees, with Pearl or alone, and watch the people, and the children playing and running. The children fish in the lake, the girls swing round the lake arm in arm, these are the older girls, they are getting off with the boys. They too walk arm in arm, stringing out across the path, and as the groups pass each other the girls laugh and cry out: Okeydoke, phone me. The little boys bring their baby sisters to the park and play with them very carefully, and see that they do not run under the railings and fall into the great lake. And they will be playing cricket, or rounders, and playing their war games. And during the war there was the Home Guard at its practice under the trees, they would be practising bring in the wounded, one man lay down flat and the other came up and got under him and put his arms (they were tied at the wrists) round his neck and so crawled off with him. And the children and the dogs were naturally very interested in this. And at the other side of the park there are the allotment people, and there is also a searchlight unit of the real army, and there is a fire practice going on at the side of the lake; the hose sucks up the water and sprays it upwards, twenty feet into the air. And at the back, in the part of the park that is railed off, there is the large house that was built by Vanbrugh, for all this parkland was once a private estate, and that is why the oak trees are so enormous and there is so little of the town park about it. This Vanbrugh house is now a hospital of recovery. The parkkeeper said to me that when he was a boy in 1880 he remembered Captain Taylor at the big house, and the red deer in the park, and how the boys of the neighbourhood were allowed to come and skate on the ice in mid-winter when the lake froze. So there is boating on the lake, too, and at the refreshment hut you may have tea, coffee, lemonade and ices, and also large slabs of cake and some bread and butter and jam.

I can see, said Caz, that every moment is occupied, it is a full rich life.

Why should it be despised, I said, by people who do not know it? I do not wish to live exactly that sort of life myself, because I have a different frame of mind; but they are happy, Caz, and we are not happy; we have not contrived to be so much as that, to be happy.

We? said Caz, questioning sadly, there is no solution for our problem, and he sat looking pale, looking at the ground.

The children, I said hurriedly, the children in our suburb, are always white-haired, blue-eyed, fat, strong children, there is, I said, a very strong nordic strain in our suburb. The highlying air of these parts is favourable to strong children. You know, Caz, I went on, when I was in Kensington Gardens one day, coming down from the Round Pond to the statue of Physical Energy by G. F. Watts, I was noticing the children of South Kensington. Now this is noticeable, once I met a crocodile of them, out walking from some high-class baby school in the neighbourhood, now these children were thin, they appeared nervous and poorly nourished, their legs were like sticks; these legs were also, a most noticeable thing, very short from knee to ankle, that is bad. They walked listlessly, in a lackadaisical manner, they wore a great mixture of garments; a little girl, for instance, was wearing a hand-woven light fawn overcoat above a longer tartan kilt, she had a fairisle knitted tam on her head, her lips were broken out in sores for the cold east wind that was blowing at that time, she seemed a boarding-school not home-cared for child you know? Her long mouse-coloured hair hung lankly in straggles, her eyes were slightly stuck out, with red lids. No, she did not look well. Some of the little boys had wind-breaker jackets and short knickers made of this expensive hand-woven material. So the children strung along, staring vacantly about them, and hanging on to the arm—those who could get near her—of a nanny-governess brisk person. This was a middle-aged girl wearing her hair in a brisk bob childishly caught up with hairslides above a weather beaten visage. As a matter of fact there were several of these grown-up persons, so that nearly all the children had someone to hang on to. These children did not compare at all favourably with the children of our suburb. For dash, durability and an alert mind they did not compare. No, Caz, they did not. Their accents were prettier of course (I do not care very much for instance for the suburban pronunciation of 'daddy'—'dur-der-ie') but languid. 'Did you and Bobby enjoy staying with Mummy?' asked the naive schoolmistress person. 'Did we enjoy staying with Lois?' poses the bored and shattered child, 'perhaps rather, she drinks a bit you know and Paul's cheque didn't come, but perhaps rather, yes; we aren't supposed to particularly.' Bobby dissociates himself from the conversation.

Caz was still looking sadly at the ground, while gently with his knees he held old Noble to an amble. I turned, swung my left leg over Noble's head, and put my arm round my cousin's neck. I am now sitting sideways, Caz's left arm is around me, his right hand lolls slackly on the rein.

So we are silent for a long time after this, and I feel very strongly the friendship of my sad cousin, that is not usually sad but laughing, and the friendship of Tiny, and the friendship of the sweet mute Heber, and I wish it might always be so, and I wish the post-war did not have to come back to us after a week, and take Caz across the sea to India, and take Tiny and me back to the Ministry. But a week is a time and a holiday. I began to laugh. I said: About our suburb, Caz—I forgot to tell you, there is also a Croquet Club.

There was now a terrific rumpus overhead, where a

Hurricane was circling in difficulties. We were near an aerodrome. There was rat-a-tat-tat from the engine and then silence, and there was a trail of exhaust smoke as the aeroplane crashed around, losing height rapidly. Suddenly fire burst out amid-riff and the Hurricane went into a spin and crashed slap into the lake from about two thousand feet.

That's done him, said Caz, looking surprised, that indeed had. Down he came into the lake, it was the first time I had seen one fall so close. The chap who was flying it also made a lake-landing and got stuck underwater with his parachute on top of him. Caz stood on the bank and hitched him out while I held Noble. The man was an escaped German prisoner, he was fearfully shook up but he took us in at a glance and spoke in English.

I, too, have been for walks, he said.

The Wandervögel type, said Caz to me.

Wander further, Vogel, I said. Caz sniggered.

Please? said our prisoner.

Not at all, said Caz.

I am a German officer, said our wet one, tightening his stance.

You're the second person I've fished out of the lake this morning, said Caz.

How do you feel? I said, but the man toppled over in a faint.

Poor old Noble, said Caz, this chap will just about finish him off.

Sighing heavily, he was going to shift him over the saddle when a company of Air Force recruits came round the lake at a brisk trot.

We left our prisoner in their charge, they were glad to have him, it was a change. We then went off to eat our sandwiches and have a sleep. Caz walked Noble home while I sat up on him dangling my feet out of the stirrups.

What a lovely day it has been, I said.

When we got home I went to look for Tiny. He was in his bedroom, at a little table by the window, crying quietly.

Oh, Tiny, I said, why are you crying now?

This time, he said, it is my brother. Oh, how he does get on my nerves. He says he is coming for the week-end, he says he wants to see Heber.

Oh, how awful, I said. Oh, Tiny, that is sufficient reason.

(Clem is this very worst sort of rich person.)

Tiny, I say, I will tell you about the first time I met Clem, it was through some pictures he had painted when he was in Istamboul. Clem said: 'We shall get on well, Celia, I feel it here.' (He is short and fat and has a theatrical habit of beating his breast—'I feel it here.')

He knew that you were a friend of mine, said Tiny, pressing his pocket handkerchief to his face, that is what he was after.

Then he said: 'Will you have a drink with me, Celia?' 'Yes, I will have a drink.'

Tiny took his face out of his handkerchief and watched me as I acted the conversation.

'I am so glad you will have a drink with me,' he says. We are in that old house of his, you know, Tiny, the one in Pont Street. 'Will you excuse me now, I have to speak to my cook; it is so sad, she is going away for the week-end, I am making the arrangements.'

As I get nearer to the idiotic, menacing, soft secret emphasizing of the unemphatic that is so much the stuff of Clem's conversation, Tiny brightens a little and, greatly daring, smiles.

So then I went into the garden. You remember Clem's roof garden in Pont Street? It is a roof garden that has the smell of cat about it, for indeed it is popular with the toms. It is also full of stone figures—putti, fawns, and of course the chimney pots. There is a madonna and child, an inferior piece of work, looted from a church at Epinal. There is also a green bronze statue that is rather good. It is the face of an old woman, it is full of doom. Underneath is written: Remember me.

Remember *Clem*—oh, if only one could forget him, but he is always there, this rich cruel crafty man, wrapped in affability; where Tiny is, there also is Clem, he is the shadow upon hope, he makes one hopeless.

Tiny hates the rich way of living, the complications and the servants, he hates that.

When I was at Clem's one day, when there was going to be an evening party, the canopy was out, the dark pink carpet was spread upon the pavement, and false green grass was laid on the tom's roof and along the covered passages.

Clem said: 'I must have my quiet time now,' and went to lie down in his room, and Cleaver, the butler, showed me to a small drawing-room at the top of the house, where there was a day-bed. So he took my shoes and left me, and the room was shut in close with heavy tapestry curtains of great value, and with expensive antique furniture. So I lay down and tried to sleep. At eight o'clock in the evening a maidservant came in with my shoes and knelt down to put them on. There was something so vile and so meek in the blond head bent over my shoes, and the mincing servant-voice asking me to raise my foot, I told her to go away, to go away quickly. . . .

I put my arms round Tiny. Tiny, I said, he cannot come

here, it is not possible. Heber will never allow it, it is not possible. For instance, Heber despises him as we do also. He cannot come.

He always comes, said Tiny, he has a sort of instinct. He is very powerful.

That is true. Clem pursues his brother to persecute him and sneer at him. He says: 'My little brother is a carpet-Communist, you know.' I have heard him say to Count Metternich before the war: 'You will find my brother very interesting, very interesting indeed, he is one of your edel-communisten.' And Count Metternich sneered too: 'You are very tolerant, you English, or very stupid, we have a way with these people in Germany, a quite different way I think.'

And so the coffin comes back from the camp, and there are the words on it to say: Do not open. How is that for the father and mother, eh, what sort of writing is that?

I am distracted thinking of the monster Clem. I run round the room, I scream: Do you remember what he did to the poet Brendan Harper, do you remember that? He took him down to stay at a rich house, and the rich man, who was a simple hunting person, was miserable for his duties as a host, which he was serious about, and not one guest could he find to set next at table to Brendan, who by this time was without one word to say. So one day the man said: 'Harper, I have found the right woman to put next to you at dinner to-night,' and he smiles with his foolish kindly smile, so Brendan at last lifted his head and said: 'Who is that?' and the host said: 'She is a most remarkable woman, she is quite remarkable, she has tired out three riding horses before breakfast.'

So after that Brendan would not come into the house at all, but he had no money, and Clem would not give him his fare home. So for the rest of the time Brendan sat outside the gates in the little niche in the wall by the keeper's lodge. And Clem was more than satisfied, for now he had a new story for his dinner parties.

Tiny was not listening, he has his own thoughts of his brother, there is no smile on his face now, he is alone.

I go out into the kitchen garden to pull some spinach for dinner. It has been raining again, it is very sloppy. I pick a basketful of spinach and come into the kitchen to help Tuffie wash it and wash the potatoes. Then I look out of the window, it is raining, it is a steady close drizzle, getting stronger, rather desperate really this terrible summertime, with the rain and the wind, and then the rain again. (But to-day the sun was out until four o'clock.)

When I was on the diabolical coast of Cornwall for my last leave I was at the Lizard, it was a farm just outside Lizard Town. There the Atlantic fog came drifting over the cliffs, and the rocks and the boulders lay with their scorched black bottoms to the heavy skies, this volcanic and terrible upheaval of the Cornish scene. And all the time it was the heavy skies, the wind and the rain, and then a great calm, and so foggy. We used to grope our way down to the bathing coves, through the fog to Church Cove, going through the cemetery, where the old church tower stood with its chest-mat of heavy ivy, and had need of it, and we used to dive off the rocks of Church Cove, guessing where the sea might be by the faint lapping of the waves against a hidden base.

I left the kitchen and walked all over Heber's house, looking into the old rooms and trailing the dark passages. It is empty, it is very old and musty. The furniture is simple, it is what one wants and no more. There is a dagger over the fire-place in the hall. There is an old chest where Uncle Heber keeps his clean surplices.

I go up the back stairs where the servants used to tread, bringing trays and coal. I am glad we have got rid of them. I detest the servant class, they are the victims and the victimizers, there is no freedom where they are. But the Tuffie idea works, that is all right, that is free.

I think of the farmhouse in Cornwall outside that Lizard Town where I stayed. Those people, that farmer and his wife, Mr. and Mrs. Truman, my word how rich they were, rich, kindly—up to a point—shrewd, and with the consumer mind, oh yes, the consumer mind that they certainly did have.

My friend and I had a sitting-room to ourselves, that was the Trumans' own drawing-room, that they let us have, but often the maid would run in to say: 'Mrs. Truman does not like you to touch the paint,' or 'Mrs. Truman does not like you to touch the radiogram,' or 'Mrs. Truman does not like the window open when it is raining.' I said to the maid: How dare you come in and touch the window when I am in here without asking my permission? I have never had to deal with so impertinent a servant as you, that will do, hold your tongue, go away. For anger runs with the servant idea. But I found that the girl was a bossy independent Cornish girl, who was doing this to show that she was no servant, but free, too free to be a bloody nuisance, so I laughed, I thought, that was over-compensating that was, I thought that was a bit too much. So later she asked us to go to a dance with her, and the anger blew away.

There was a mattress on top of a chest of drawers over by the stairhead outside Uncle's room in this fine old rectory, so I lay out flat there for a bit, laughing as I remembered the furniture at our Cornish farm, that was furnished in the richest fancies of Tottenham Court Road, with a fine panto-baronial look about the chocolate brown painted panelling, the heavy sideboard, the complicated mantelshelf and the high-up fretwork friezes. The cusions were ruched silk in royal blue, old gold and crimson.

So thinking of these two houses, the rectory and the farm, and the difference there is between them, and the way the farmhouse costs so much, and the rectory so little, I fell into a comfortable doze.

After supper it is night and the moon stands high in the night sky. The whole night is very calm, and the rain has cleared, the air is soft and warm.

I see Uncle Heber starting out for the church, he has his coat on and his muffler hanging round his neck. I go with him, holding his hand, this sad silent and loving person. He is a noble animal of integrity, like his sister, my Aunt, he is this honest person. I do not say anything.

When we get into the church Uncle goes up to the altar to change the cloth or the frontals, or something. I kneel down in the aisle, leaning back on my heels with my head against the pew, I say: The soul does not grow old, the soul sees everything and learns nothing, and I say: How can we come back to God, to be taken into Him, when we are so hard and so separate and do not grow, after we are fifteen we do not grow or change. And I say, if we are to be taken back, oh why were we sent out, why were we sent away, why were we sent away from God? And I see the moonlight coming down through the queer sepia windows, for this church has these queer sepia windows that are like the windows of Magdalen College chapel, and the sepia figures look sad and I begin to cry, oh how forlorn the moonlight looks, shining through sepia. And I think

116

of Tom, of my uncle's mad son Tom, and wish for comfort I was in his arms again, and much comfort that should be, it is not in Tom's arms that comfort lies. In whose arms, then, in whose arms may comfort lie, is it permitted?

Uncle begins to pray out loud and to say the psalms for the evening. It is the twenty-eighth evening of the month. I hear my gentle uncle saying softly the psalms for the evening: 'Blessed shall he be that taketh thy children; and throweth them against the stones.'

I sit back and lean my head against the pew in the shadow beside the moonlight and I remember how I was talking about the psalms with Tom one day, and he said it was a pity if ever the church was no longer allowed to take the children, so that never were they able to hear and learn the prayer book psalms that are often so much more beautiful than the bible psalms, and I said that I had the pick-rag mind that was full of tags of the church, and the classics, but that was well enough as far as it went, and had served me well enough, and further into it I did not wish to go, I guessed I had come off light.

Tom and I were having our talk in a Greek restaurant and I tried to spell out the Greek notices, but even the Greek alphabet was by now filmy to me. And I said how girls were better off than the boys in the way they came late to the Greek and ran quickly at it, and already in my first term at Greek I was translating the Alcestis into the terrible school-child jargon; and I said, I now remember the jargon, it was, O halls of Admetus in which I god though I was suffered to endure menial toil for Zeus was responsible hurling thunderbolts at the chest of my son Aesculapius.

And Tom said it was different with boys, this classical idea, and it was a burden and a misery and an outrage, and that twice was he flogged through Homer, and that the reason

117

girls did not advance so far was that at girls' schools there was no corporal punishment and that it was only the fear of pain that would drive these bored and wretched children to their tasks.

But I think there might be one good thing that would come out of it, and for that one good thing the years and tears of boredom must pay, for in a general way that is often how it is, so that if we had not had that we should not have this, for all the wastage and lossage. But that is a poor hang-dog argument, we should hurry up to find a better way, and it was certainly at school, in my grand second school after I had left behind my dear kindergarten, that I first learnt to be bored and to be sick with boredom, and to resist both the good with the bad, and to resist and be of low moral tone and non-co-operative, with the 'Could do Better' for ever upon my report and the whole of the school-girl strength going into this business of resistance, this Noli-me-tangere, this Come near and I shoot.

There is dead sea fruit in the schoolchild's mouth, and Africa and her deserts in the hair on her head. And there is the feeling of guilt in the schoolchild's mind, and she turns her head this way and that and cries: 'Now it is over, now it will soon be over.'

Uncle has now finished the psalms and he asks me to choose a hymn, to sing it, so I sing:

> Ride on, ride on in majesty,
> In lowly pomp ride on to die;
> Bow Thy meek head to mortal pain,
> Then take, O Lord, Thy power and reign.

But I sing the last line under my breath, for I do not see Christ in glory, but only upon the Cross. So we come back in company hand in hand, together, without a word spoken.

X

THIS MORNING I have had a letter from the Ministry, from Harley, to say that Harley has bought a canary, this little bird is a great singer, he is called Hoofa. Harley is worried about Hoofa's diet, what is he to be fed on? He has some mixture he bought with Hoofa at Harrods, but is it the best, is this mixture the best he can do for his bird? Is there not some special shop, the Claridge's of bird shops, where Hoofa's needs may be fitly met?

So Harley sends me a copy of *Feathered Friends*, and I spend the morning on long-distance calls to London. So then I write a long letter to Harley to tell him what I have done, and how many of the many shops I have rung up, and how many of them have been bombed to bits and are no longer there.

I also send Harley a cutting from the *Louth Recorder*, which quotes the following citation of honour, and says: 'V.C. Pigeon Demobilized', and goes on to say that the Carrier Pigeon Ten-Year-Old-Mercury has been given the Dicken Medal and that this is the highest award for gallantry that a bird or an animal can get, and that it was given to Mercury for a flight from Denmark to Louth with an important message from the Danish Underground.

So then it is twelve o'clock and I think I have done some hard work, and I go out to muck about in the mud by the river bank. And I brush my hand to my eyes, for I have the thought that Harley was wishing to take a tug at my long so-long holiday-long leash and to let me know that I am not quit of him, of London, of the Ministry, of the job, the job.

Whatever the High Ones want I have this Under-discipline *Zu-Befehl* feeling, this I-get-it-for-you Universal-aunt, Dog-with-nose-to-trail Ah-Ariel Gefühl (ah, when shall I be free?).

At the Ministry, Rackstraw envied Harley his fine dog Day. Day was a pale blond retriever, a loving nervous dog, a fine gun dog, too, was she. So when Harley could not keep Day any longer, by reason of giving up his house and taking a flat, he gave her away to a friend who was often shooting. But the old man Rackstraw grieved over Day going away like that, and said how cruel it was, when Day was this loving sensitive dog, to send her off.

But I said it was much crueller if Harley had kept her cooped up in a London flat. So Rackstraw sighed and said: Yes, he supposed so. But, oh, I could see how much he hankered after that beautiful dog that was now gone away. But I would not have it said that Harley was cruel, why no, why, he was the most animal-loving man you could find, himself every evening oversaw the preparation of Day's evening meal.

So then to cheer poor Rackstraw who was grown quite melancholy because of his loving thought for the dog Day, I told him the story of a dog-loving family in my home suburb who gave their dog to the Army to be trained for the front line duties, but for some reason or other, maybe it was one dog too many for them, this dog after his training was complete was sent home to his family owners. So I remember now, it was an injury to his right fore-paw, he was invalided out. So home he came. But this dog had been taught fierce ways and an untamed behaviour, he had been taught that he must bite and fight, and to bite for death, so he knew where to bite all right, he had been taught again his wolf behaviour; so when his loving master went to meet him, coming down the garden path to the garden gate with the rest of the family where he was coming in, the dog ran forward and leaped up, his fangs were bared, he went to bite the throat out of his loving friend. So the man warded him off, with his heavy stick the old man clubbed him down, so the dog died and they buried him in the back garden with feelings of sorrow, and on his gravestone they wrote: 'He Died for King and Country.'

This story lifted the dark mood of Rackstraw and he began to hum and sing, and when at that moment a friend rang him up on the telephone, he was as gay as a bird, and when he was hanging up he said in his own gay way: God bless you and the Pope of Rome. So the mood passed.

And so, thinking of this and that, I roamed the park and the river bank; and as I walked the grass track between the trees, I saw Tiny coming towards me. He looked well and happy, except for his limp, for he still walked lame, his leg and left side had been badly burnt when he was shot down in his aeroplane.

Why, Tiny, I said, how well and happy you look, have you perhaps heard that Clem after all is not coming, that he is prevented?

Yes, he said, he is prevented.

I did not ask how. Had Heber put his foot down? But I did not believe that that would prevent Clem. As a matter of fact I did not absolutely believe that Clem was prevented, but I did not say so. At least he was not with us at the moment, and that, when you are thinking of Clem, is always at least something.

So I walked with Tiny, strolling arm-in-arm with him

along the sandy river path. Presently he pointed to the lake: *C'est le lac de Jeudi*, he said. Then he said with an ineffable soft smile: You see, it is Thursday to-day.

Tiny is broken, he is a broken man, I love Tiny, but there is too much pity in this love, there is something of that, it is not altogether a feeling that one human being should have for another. So I break arms with Tiny and go off alone.

Tiny lay down to sleep on a bank by the river by a willow tree. I went a long way off and began to wade in the mud and out into the shallow water to watch the grubs floating on the quiet water and to see the fish go by.

I wished Tom was with me with his fishing tackle, this brimming rich Ouse is rich in fish. Eh, what a foolish thought, what use is Tom? Let Tom rest in childhood memories, a fishing boy, a conversation friend, a hunter of eagles' nests, my shadow cousin that is now grown man and lost his wits, mad Tom.

I remember the long summer days of childhood that are such a pleasure, nothing is ever such a pleasure again, tired and hot and happy the hours come to teatime.

Well, the childhood days have come again for me in this way, I will not be burdened by the convention of politeness, I will not go back to Tiny, to take his arm and draw him back to the rectory for tea. Oh, will I not? So I think I will not, do I?

Politeness is too strong; I go back to Tiny, to the stricken broken Tiny, wretched brother of a wretched Clem. On the way back with him I talk feverishly about Lopez, making it up as we go along.

Oh, Tiny, I say, I was round at your sister's the other day, I had brought my drawings to get some advice. Lopez was standing by the table with a worried look, the table had the usual typewriter on it and a lot of crumbs, also a half-eaten melon, a jug of burnt cocoa and some pieces of bread and butter and a tin of Australian plum jam with the jam in a splodge on the tumbled tablecloth, you know? She was singing, too, what an irritating girl. 'I don't know which to put on,' she said, turning to me, she had a red turban twisted round her head. She had on her bustbodice, a rucked-up vest, some aertex drawers. (So I built up the picture, I was getting quite warmed to it by now, oh, how I relish this picture.) What goes well with Lopez, I said, is that sort of underwear. A glance at the high-class ladies' papers with their headache captions—each caption is a headache, I knew a girl who worked on 'em—puts one off the other sort, my word it does. One fancies honest underclothes. Lopez was looking rather comical—which one shall I put on? You know, Tiny, I hate the fashion girl with her famous old fashion slant. It is fashion, fashion, fashion all the way. Evidently a person of discrimination, ahem. Oh, leave it, leave it, you horrible fashion girl, be careless, lively, negligent and dirty. I love grubby girls, Tiny, with the hair in their eyes, and the pastel-coloured features screwed in absurd concentration. The fashion slant is smug, careful, sly, furtive and withholding. 'Which shall I put on?' is the girl I like. So Lopez is playing all the time, not serious really, but only comic-serious in concentration—'you will tell me.' So I laugh, too, and tell her to tie the red one properly and keep that one on. That will slay him, I say, that will fetch him away. For it is of Winsome Elliott her darling that she is now thinking.

With all this talk of Lopez, Tiny has now forgotten the painful incident of *Le lac de Jeudi*, so we part in friendship and go to our rooms, we can now meet friendlily at supper and go on where we left off. In my bedroom I sigh, thinking, how long must that go on?

The girl Lopez has no sense of religious feelings, she thinks that religion is a political idea, an idea to be convenient for the power types to suppress the lowly. But not Winsome Elliott himself nor all his dialectical materialists has ever struck off the sentence that I see in my bedroom writ up over my head. There is first the picture of a great brown whale creature swimming in an oleographic green sea, very vast and swelling, and across this picture is printed in letters of gold and crimson, *Did You Make Leviathan?* There it is, rather faded by now, stuck up over my bed. Did You Make Leviathan?

I think that the intellectuality of Winsome, that runs also in Lopez, runs mostly with the twenty-to-fifty years of man, and that the *instinctuality*, that brings with it so much glee, so much pleasure that cannot be told, so much of a vaunting mischievous humility, so much of a truly imperial meekness, runs with childhood and old age; and as I am by nature of this type of person, it is perhaps because I now run in these *middle* years that I am not enjoying it but must cast ever backwards to my childhood and forwards to my old age. It is the writer John Cowper Powys who has this fullest free feeling of the pleasures of *instinctuality*, the fleering humble cold fish that he is, the wily old pard of the rocks and the stones, the Welsh carp fish in his British pool.

The feeling of full enjoyment will flood in again, we must get through these middle years.

When we come down to the warm untidy supper kitchen the sky has clouded over again, it is so dark and sulphurous we put the candles on the table.

We are all dirty and muddy and tired. Caz has been off shooting somewhere, Heber has been digging potatoes, his finger nails are black, his head is sunk on his breast. Tiny also has not washed, his fair soft hair hangs over his eyes. My legs are muddy and the skin feels soft from the river water.

Caz sees that there has been something happening between Tiny and me, he is in a malicious mood and says softly in my ear, so that Heber shall not hear the forbidden name—he wishes Tom was here.

So do I, I said. This kitchen would not then be a place I should wish to leave.

Pass the whisky, said Caz.

The conversation now got into politics. Caz gave me a malicious look and said: We should quit India, that is what we should do, there is nothing else for us to do but that; we should quit India.

It is not so simple as that, I said, passing a filthy handkerchief across my mouth. The rest of the world is very unanimous to say the English should quit India, Palestine, Malaya, the Antarctic and South Africa; but why, please? Why should the world, with none too clean a forefinger, point out the path of sainthood for England to follow, while they go quite another way themselves?

Oh, said Caz, it is an excuse, of course, they are so bored, really, just to go on seeing England there, it is getting boring for them, they think: That survival lump, it's about time we shifted her.

Just to make a change, eh? Just a nice change, let's go to Margate this year, mum, it will make a change, something like that I suppose? I said.

Something rather like that, you know, said Caz, those infernal islanders, ahem, something like that.

And their own social habits, these Indians, they are so pretty I suppose and so practical, eh? Burn the widows, rape the kids, up the castes, and hurrah for Indian legal probity.

That's the spirit, said Caz, pass the whisky.

The English law is above the world, I said, it is not to be bought, it is strong, flexible and impartial.

Caz began to sing: The law is the embodiment, Of everything that's excellent, It has no kind of spot or flaw, And I my Lords embody the law. And this new whipping law, this Emergency Whipping Act they have passed for India?

It is this inflammable student material, I said, wringing my hands, for indeed I felt it to be a shameful thing. It was a horrible necessity, I said, pleading with Caz. Surely for instance it is better than Shoot-the-boys?

Oh, yes, much better, said Caz, because you can do it several times. It is always such fun. I remember how I used to enjoy it so much at school, we always had this clean wholesome fun, we derived great pleasure from it, eh, Tiny?

Tiny look away. I think there's a great deal of nonsense talked about this flogging business at public schools, he said. After all, what is it, nothing.

You did not use to think so, said Caz.

That's the spirit, I said, pass the whisky. The British will always eventually pass flogging laws because the governing classes are flogged themselves so much through the public schools.

I was flogged twice through Homer, said Caz with another malicious look in my direction.

I agree with Tiny, I said in a desperate manner, too much is made of it, some men writers make so much of it as some women writers will always be making of the stress and strain of childbirth.

Well, that cannot be so easily removed.

126

It was a vile thing, I cried, a vile thing. But it was a vile thing that such a vile thing should have been forced upon us by the abysmal childishness of the Indians, who are like the young man of Thermopylae, who never did anything properly. Did the bloody fools think it was not to put a spoke in the allies' wheel, did they not think that? did they suppose that in doing that they were not fighting for Hitler? It was enough to make a cat laugh, with a grin that stretched from Tokio to Berlin.

That's the spirit, said Caz, pass the whisky.

It was very much the situation that the Romans had with Christ, said Tiny primly.

Oh, go on, Tiny, please go on, said Caz.

Tiny flushed and said: Well, I mean. . . .

I said: It *was* the same, the Romans crucified Christ.

And we made a stooge of Gandhi.

I said: This Gandhi now, he was comfortably held in an expensive bungalow, while his non-violent followers, fallen into violence and destruction. . . .

And being very properly beaten for it, said Caz.

I think the Congress leaders did a crafty thing, they made a false assault, it was a political feint, they must I suppose for one little minute have had to be afraid that the English might have given them what they wanted, and what then? Then they would have had the responsibility, and the possibility—the certainty—of failing and being discredited; but now you see, they stand by their assault, they went to prison, they not they were not beaten, and now the war is over they present themselves as heroes that have been put on ice for the duration.

That's the spirit, said Caz, pass the beer.

We had now finished the whisky. But all the time at the back of my mind is the thought of the expedient crucifixion, the crucifixion of Christ by the Romans, by the governing Romans, and I thought of England again and of the voices against her, and how they are saying that England should go because she no longer governs; they say she does not govern, that she is like water shifting to her own course, that she is not strong like Rome. Oh, is she not? Is not this an envious and superficial argument? And I sighed again and thought of those voices against England and I thought of the poem I wrote called by this name, *Voices against England in the Night:*

England, you had better go,
There is nothing else that you ought to do,
You lump of survival value, you are too slow.

England, you have been here too long,
And the songs you sing now are the songs you sung
On an earlier day, now they are wrong.

And as you sing the sliver slips from your lips
And the governing garment sits ridiculously on your hips
It is a pity you are still too cunning to make slips.

Dr. Goebbels, that is the point,
You are a few years too soon with your jaunt,
Time and the moment is not yet England's daunt.

Yes, dreaming Germany, with your Urge and Night
You must go down before English and American might,
It is well, it is well, cries the peace kite.

Perhaps England our darling will recover her lost thought,
We must think sensibly about our victory and not be dis-
    traught,
Perhaps America will have an idea, and perhaps not.

But they cried, Could not England once the world's best
Put off her governing garment and be better dressed
In a shroud, a shroud. Oh, history turn thy pages fast.

And I said to Caz: We are leaving India, you know that
we are leaving India. All that we have now been saying is
already in the past, we are leaving India. It is a thing beyond
thought in the world's history, it is the first time since men
grew to cities and government, the first time that a great
Power in the full flush of the greatest victory that men have
won, it is the first time that such a Power has taken its
vassal country, its under-nation for three hundred years in
liege, and given it freedom; it is the first time a great
colonizing Power, not driven by weakness but in strength
choosing to go, has walked out for conscience sake and for
the feeling that the time has come. That is the answer to
the voices in the night.

Tiny began to hum 'There is a green hill far away', and
broke into the words as they came back to him:

> There is a green hill far away
> Without a city wall
> Where our dear Lord was crucified
> Who died to save us all.

All right, Tiny, said Caz, that was the usual sentence,
you know, how many Jews were crucified by Titus outside
the walls of Jerusalem, eh? How many thieves and vagabonds
perished on the cross? The Romans said that Medicine
Cross was the best remedy for Jewish obstinacy, we seem
to have heard echoes of this in our own times. It was a
perfectly legal sentence, codified and open, the criminals
knew that they stood to be crucified, after trial the sentence.

Oh, yes, I said, and looked at the tablecloth, the yellow pattern was faded in the wash. I said: The law allows it and the court awards.

Yes, said Caz, and with the flogging sentence, too, there is precedent and trial and the flogging judge has his flogging look. The law allows it and the court awards.

I began to think of the cruelty and inflexibility of human law, I thought of the corrupt Cenci trial, the old sour Pope wielding his power for the old bad murdered father, that had committed so many sins, compounding with his gold for sodomy, that on that charge alone should have been burnt at the stake. And I thought of Gibbon, 'The graver charges were mercifully waived and the Vicar of Christ stood accused only of murder, rape, incest and sodomy'. And I thought that Shakespeare had caught in a phrase the cruelty and blindness of the world and of history, 'the law allows it, and the court awards' (with the Cenci postscript that harsh law can be made yet worse by private arrangement).

But not in England, I cried, at least the English law cannot be bought.

That is true, said Caz, at least not by the poor, and also it is true of course that it is not quite so harsh as the medieval code. Pass the beer.

There was silence now for a time while we helped ourselves to the raspberries and took the top off the milk for cream.

When you've quite finished, Tiny, said Caz.

There is a bitter taste in my mouth, I feel that I have been très Blimp, presque cad, that Caz is superficial and in a spiteful mood. Always there are these under-tugs and cross currents, nothing is simple, nothing to be settled.

Tiny also looks sad.

When Tiny was walking along the lake path with me

I knew that he was thinking of Vera Hennessey. For Vera, we all know, he has had this sentimental feeling that has lasted for years and eaten away at him. It is contrary to his political feelings. But oh, what sort of strength have Tiny's political feelings, what sort of strength at all has Tiny? In between times he gets tied up with girls, always in rather an unhappy way, and always he comes back to Vera. Tiny shows me the letters he has from her. She is a great girl for writing letters, they are absolutely nauseating. These two call each other by terrible pet names, as if Tiny itself was not already enough. I know Vera well, but all the same he has to show me her photograph. I remember Harley's comment about Vera:'What a wet little thing, there's a good deal of bed in that face, if only she'd wipe the drip off the end of her nose.'

Oh, Tiny, how you do go on, I thought, how tedious your affections, how ridiculous you are, and how hard you work to make something of nothing. Oh, the fights and ecstasies of the spirit, and the sad pursuing bones. Now, that is enough.

Vera was lunching with me one day. She said: My maid has sent me out without my lipstick, she'll be sending me out without my dress next.

Tiny looked at her photograph and said: 'There is music in that face, and lakewater and sunset.' Well, Tiny, it might be Charles Morgan, it might be Sparkenbroke.

I am now well through my raspberries and cream. I look towards Uncle Heber and I say: We are among corrupt people, how can we be innocent? How can we have a revolution and make a new world when we are so corrupt?

He does not answer. I turn furiously upon Tiny: You ought to be stuffed up with carrot, I say. He begins to cry.

131

I don't love men, he says, I love women, but it is never right, it is never happy.

Why have I said such a cruel thing to Tiny? It is because I am unhappy. I wish to be alone with Uncle Heber and quit of the two of them. I crumble some bread.

Do not waste the bread, Celia, says my Uncle, then he says: There is a parcel that has come for you, it is on the sideboard.

Oh, yes, I say, it is the Swiss wrist watch I got for Tiny's birthday last week.

Tiny, I say, this is the wrist watch I got for your birthday, it took time coming through, here it is.

I took it to him at the end of the table and strapped it round his wrist; his old wrist watch had got broken on a rock, he forgot to take it off when he was bathing, and crawling out of the pool he smashed it straight off against the rock; it was in Cornwall.

You will find that this one will go when you are under water.

When I am under water, said Tiny, and looked very pleased.

Many happy returns of last Monday, I said, and came back to my seat.

Caz began to talk in a literary way about the Emperor Claudius. He, it seems, was in a corrupt society.

I do not know whether you are talking about the Claudius of the history books and the research material, or about the Claudius of Robert Graves, I say, but that is the only Claudius I know.

My cousin and I share an admiration for Graves's Claudius, so that the atmosphere is becoming a little more agreeable. I do not really care how much Robert Graves has made up his Claudius, because his Claudius is alive, alive-o, with his troubles and his tears and his humiliations, and his mind that is subtle, honest and stubborn.

The terrible grandmother, I say, the terrible Livia, with her noose round her husband's neck. Yes, Tiny, you see the great Augustus was impotent, with his wife he could have no intercourse, Livia used this as a weapon, she ruled him, she kept the noose round his neck, and jerked the cord, every now and then she jerked it tight. How was that, do you think? And the little boy Claudius grew up, he was a sort of cripple, and he grew up with his tutor and his books and his stammer. (Tiny has to be told, he does not know.) And the lady fiend his grandmother broke what would have been a happy marriage for him, and married him off to a great laughing-stock of a girl, who hated him and was always sulky-silent. How do you think that was? You leave women alone, Tiny, you're well off as you are.

How you do exaggerate, Celia, said Caz.

Well, better off, then.

Caz folded his hands sententiously and said: The better is the enemy of the good.

Shut up, Caz.

How did it go, the Claudius business? said Tiny, who was quite cheerful again by now, with his keen gossip-column nose a-quiver for news.

Well, I said, to be perfectly candid, it did not go at all well.

To begin with, said Caz, knowing what Tiny wanted and maliciously steering away from it, to begin with, Claudius entertained the very highest hopes of reform. He worked hard, he was talented, industrious and methodical, he knew that if he could not succeed, nobody could.

And he did not succeed, I said. And he knew that it was hopeless, for he did not underrate himself to think some-one else could have made a better job of it. So he said that only corruption could cure corruption, and he married Messalina. and he gave the inheritance not to his son

133

Britannicus, who had been raised in Britain in innocent circumstances, but to Nero Drusillius Germanicus. So he thought: Let them have corruption, let them have Nero, and he knew that Messalina would poison Britannicus, and she did. And he knew that Messalina would also poison him, and he hoped it wouldn't be long. So in the end she did, and it wasn't, and so he died too.

It wasn't Messalina who did that, said Caz, it was his third wife. Caz turned to Tiny. She was young, he said, young and as bad as they make 'em, and Claudius was an old doting man, and Graves makes up this sad couplet to show how sad it was for them:

There is no sound so laughable, so laughable and sad
As an old man weeping for his wife, a girl gone to the bad.

Oh, the terrible corrupt people, I said, thinking of the Phaidon Roman Portraits that are so corrupt and so con-temporary in appearance, there had to be a war, what else can there be when people are so corrupt? How in govern-ment can we keep the simplicity and the innocence, how can we do that? People govern, they are knaves, they are governed, they are simpletons.

Looking out for Number One, says Caz.

Yes, that is what the Roman Portraits should be called, that is what they are like.

Tuffie came in with a copy of the *Evening Standard* she had picked off the pantry shelf. It was six years old. Look at this, she said, here's a picture of old Churchill on Wapping Steps the time they got the shelter, takes you back, doesn't it?

Caz took the paper and turned it over and read a bit to himself and then read it out loud. This bit said that Laval had handed some Jewish refugees to the Germans, to the Gestapo.

134

Caz went on to say what the Polish communist government had just now done to the man who had worked for him under the German Occupation of Poland.

I ran to Uncle Heber, who was crying quietly at his end of the table. I knelt down and pulled his hands away from his face: Do not cry for what Laval did, do not cry, Uncle Heber.

Caz came down upon us in a sudden fury, he had the *Evening Standard* in his hand.

There will always be people, he said, who will advance themselves by licking the bleeding piles of Louis XIV.

Tiny, I screamed, Tiny. You should say: Caz, may I knock you down?

Caz tried to pull me away from Heber. I looked up into Heber's face, I said: *Je ne peux pas le voir que sur la croix.*

He must have been glad to die, said Caz.

No, no, it was not suicide, it was not the end, it could not have been the end.

Heber smiled at me in a solemn friendly way, he said: *Tu seras punie par où tu as tant péché.* Then he said: *Dans ton cœur frivole.*

I started to scream: No, no. At this moment there was a crash as the chimney pot blown off by the gale that had got up fell on the outhouse. In the light of the fire that started up, as it had dropped on to some petrol cans standing on the outhouse roof, I saw two figures riding up to the house on bicycles.

It is Mabel and Kathie, I said, I forgot they were coming to supper, and now we have eaten the supper.

We rushed for the pails and pumps.

Mind the sandbags, said Tiny, as we crashed out of the side door.

Bring them along, you fool, said Caz.

What a lucky thing we never dug them into the asparagus beds, I said.

The terrible boredom that followed must now be described. Kathie insisted on playing bridge, and Mabel does not play.

For half an hour I escaped to go and get them some more supper. I scrambled them some dried eggs with some cheese, and made them a salad and made some coffee and took as long a time over it as I could, which is very long.

There was then another respite while Mabel and Kathie ate their eggs and we all helped drink the coffee. We pushed the bottles under the mangle, as Kathie dislikes strong drink.

I was thinking that it is only sometimes that I am topdog over Kathie, and only then for a short time, as it was the day she told me she was coming to stay with Mabel.

This old girl Kathie has such stoutness and strength, she outruns me quite, on a long stretch she does this, yes, in the long run I am subservient to Kathie, she rules me. So when she says: We will have some bridge, with a warning severe look, I know that, however much I may resist, that in fact is what we shall have. So we do.

Our bridge is the auction-family-variety. Why didn't you play the ace? Well, I don't know, I thought you were leading from the King. But Tuffie bids hearts. Oh, yes.

Caz and Tiny of course will not play, Kathie has no hold over them. They went at once, going together friendly like for once, united in escape. So Tuffie loves bridge, Tuffie will play, and Heber plays for politeness sake, but he plays a good game.

Really, Celia, why you let Kathie have the call with that hand, I cannot imagine.

Doesn't it go round again? I say. Well, I only bid a club

to open it up and let Kathie know what to lead, well, can't I go No Trumps now? No. So we made five diamonds. Oh, heaven, and people play for hours. The clock hand has now crept round to eleven.

Won't you have some tea before you go, Kathie? I'm sure Mabel would like some tea.

Kathie falters, she is lost, yes, Mabel would like some tea.

It is funny when we are at home to see Kathie and my sister Pearl together, they are cat and dog, they are fighting mad. Pearl does not budge one inch, Kathie does not budge one inch, it is battle drawn and equal. But Kathie is fond of me, she loves me, she is a governessy loving person, to me she is like this. 'You had better change your shoes, Celia, you feet are wet.' Et cetera.

So I go and make the tea and bring it in, and surely that is the end of the bridge. But no, Tuffie is now mad to finish the rubber. Oh, Tuffie, once fast friend to me, false fleeting perjured Clarence, oh, heaven, and now some more.

We go on playing, and now it is twelve o'clock, it is midnight. I can only remember one thing to make me laugh, it was the newspaper criticism of Hamlet, they said that Mr. Snooks played the King as if in momentary apprehension that somebody else would play the Ace. I begin to laugh.

Kathie rises and says they really must go. It is now a clear starry night and I go to the door with them, and Kathie and Mabel kiss me and I say: Thank you for coming and thank you for the game.

Kathie gives me a green silk purse, she says: I made you this green silk purse for your birthday, I may not be home for your birthday, so I will wish you many happy returns of the day with this green silk purse.

Oh, not a green silk purse, I say. Oh, Kathie, that is just what I wanted.

It will match your green felt hat, when the autumn comes, says Kathie.

Good-bye. Good-bye. They go off in a loving way, wobbling a little down the drive on their bicycles because of the cart ruts and the sloppy moss. Good-bye.

Heber, I say, kneeling on the hearth mat beside him, was it all right, did it go all right?

Well, it was a façade with chips.

But they did not notice?

Well, no, as a matter of fact I think they did not take a look to notice.

When my mama and my aunt were girls, when your little sisters were at home and you were away at school, they were called down from bed often to play whist with grandfather, how was that I wonder?

Well, they were unselfish, loving girls, and they were brought up to think of others.

Oh, yes, that is how it is, one has to be brought up to it. You know, Uncle, the pain of the boredom is actual, and yet it was only three hours. My mama and my aunt must have had three hours many nights running. (I sighed to think of it, I sighed for them.)

Then I said: As a matter of fact, my mama and my aunt adored whist, it was for them the greatest pleasure. So we go on to talk of something else.

XI

THE NEXT day at breakfast there is a review in the
paper of a book by another American general about
the war and how awful the British are. Oh, Caz, I say,
look here, not another one. Oh, look here, oh, I say. . . .

Oh, do shut up, do be quiet, oh, Lord.

It's the chip on the shoulder, I went on, the way they have
to be mean about England, oh, heavens, why do they have
to go on like this (the reviewer was hitting hard), well,
look, they can be generous, affectionate, cocky, plucky and
so on, but about England they have to be mean. It is like a
rich woman who has everything she wants except her
husband's love. So she hits him over the head with the frying
pan and says, Love me. Oh, heavens, Caz, what we did
not have to put up with in the war from this nag-pot ally
of ours. And yet there is something of envy in it, too,
as if they wanted to despise us and yet wanted to be like
us, too, it is a bit of a puzzle I must say. We are always
very generous to them, aren't we? Why, look, all the
victories were always reported as American victories, we
gave 'em Radar and the Merlin and penicillin and most
of the atom bomb . . . and who bust the Moehne dam . . .
and pin-pointed that gaol in Lille? . . . it must be those
damned lying school histories of theirs, and the War of
Independence. But didn't they win that, so why so sore
about it? And weren't they all British anyway, until after

it was over? . . . Well, we ought to say, America, England is not the enemy, concentrate on those Russkies. . . .

Thanking Heaven for them, Caz snapped.

. . . keep tabs on them, stop looking under the bed, for a soldier in red. Not that they don't; keep tabs on the Russians, I mean . . . oh, heck. And not that I don't like the Americans, I do, and not that I don't like their language, why look how . . . oh, heck. Oh, why do they have to go on in this terrible dreary way?

Oh, there is no answer, said Caz, who was reading a technical paper on ballistics, oh, just don't take any notice of it. Why don't you go and find Tiny?

Well if he can't come down and get his breakfast, why should I?

But the terrible nagging spirit of the American general's book as it comes at me through the reviewer's tart comments is eating away at me. I fling about rather, remembering the moods of guilt and uncertainty that were the war moods of the period before D-Day. Oh, how strongly it comes back, oh, why did we present the news so badly, making it seem always that the worst was happening, with no word of vigour and comfort?

I remember, Caz, when the news came through about the British Commando raid, it was stated that the raid would be a tonic for the American public, headlines from the American papers were given, 'U.S.A. troops invade the Continent,' 'We invade the Continent,' etc. Lord Lovat told me. . . .

Lord Lovat told you, cried Caz, dipping his paper. *I* told you.

He reached for the marmalade.

There is no marmalade for breakfast, but there is some South African Green Plum jam in the tin.

This feeling of making a bad case is eating away at me. It will be our undoing, I say, we shall be ruined.

This country is finished, jeered Caz, haven't you forgotten that bit?

Well, I said, we should speak up for ourselves. A very nice American was speaking to me the other day, he said: You British ('you Bri-ish') ought to speak up for yourselves. I agree, well, why don't we, I say?

Why should we bother?

Caz, you make me sick. The trouble with this country is that everybody is just bone lazy. England is a country given over to sloth.

Tiny came into the room in his dressing gown and sat down in Heber's place.

I don't think I'll have any breakfast this morning.

The porridge is in the pan on the kitchen fire.

Tiny took his plate and spoon and went out.

Take the victory, Caz, I said, our very laziness made us come to it in the end with so much the more terrible slow strength. It is what the German professor said about England: 'It is a pity in the end there must be this slow accumulation of a steady and ferocious impetus, there will be very little left when she has done.'

Without that slow accumulation of ferocious impetus, said Caz, it is very probable there wouldn't have been any victory. The Blitz-Krieg was their card, it was played and beaten.

... The Canadians, I went on, so glad after years of long training, the brilliant Lord Lovat, his brilliant Commandos, the buoyant spirit. The news was tarnished, I said, it is always tarnished.

After breakfast I go and help Uncle to dig potatoes.

Uncle, I say, I think sloth is a terrible sin, it is a special sin of mine, is it not? and it runs with fear. Yes, with my sin of sloth there runs also the sin of fear; the sluggard saith: There is a lion in the way, a lion is in the street. It is fear and mistrust, fear of action and so inaction. I could never marry because of fear, I should like to have one-third of a man, to be the third wife, perhaps, with her own house—*einverstanden*, it is difficult to share a kitchen— but to be the one wife, that is the dear one and the comfort, to be the dear one and the comfort of one man, that I admire, that I could not dare to be, I should be afraid there was a lion in the street. Uncle, I am not proud of this, it is not right or natural. Uncle, you see how it is. (I begin to cry, the tears fall down into the potato trench.) Uncle, there is a man who is after me, he was married, he is not married now. I admired his wife, she had so much courage, she was very capable. That sounds cold, but it is not. It is absolutely necessary to be practical. And she was practical.

Uncle does not know that it is of Tom I am speaking, of his own son; he does not know that for me to marry Tom might be a way out for both of us, perhaps. But there also is fear, that is where fear also speaks.

Uncle, I say, I was reading the Proverbs last night, what I just quoted, they are very practical, but in some fashion also they make an unpleasant picture of a too practical, too self-advantageous virtue. The ones that are repeated so often, you know? Don't waste time talking to fools, don't chatter, don't go after strange women, don't stay in bed. Be a squirrel, be an ant, the improvident person shall have nothing to eat in the winter. Don't spare the rod, beat your children, beat sense into your little ones, etc. And above all, don't back bills for strangers. There is, of course, this real noble love of wisdom, this is very strong, but it is so often the wisdom of Polonius, 'looking out for Number One'.

Uncle, a lot of gay and generous people, like Lopez for instance, chatter an awful lot, and borrow money, and are not ants or squirrels. It is necessary to be practical. But it is not the whole of wisdom, it is not, it is only a part. Everything in this world is in fits and splinters, like after an air raid when the glass is on the pavements; one picks one's way and is happy in parts. Uncle, one sometimes has the false thought that if one could go back to one's childhood, right back as far as was possible, one should say: Here I first began to be wrongly educated, here I first was going wrong, here I went along the wrong path. And so the thought springs up, very forceful, very strong: Ah, if I could get back to that point, now that I know what I do know, it would be different. But really I know that it would not, I remember the poem I wrote, it had the line, 'Prenatally biassed, grow worser, born bad'. Yes, Uncle, everything is different but everything is always the same.

My tears fall down so fast I cannot see the potatoes.

Oh, I say, if we were meant to come back to God, why were we sent out, why were we sent away? I wish for innocence more than anything, but I am conscious only of corruption. You know it is the way now to decry the trivial mind of Aldous Huxley, but he has indeed found some wise poems to put in his anthology, he has found some true things to say about the corrupt heart; he loves innocence, too, and seeks it out, but is conscious of corruption. You know, Uncle, some people are born with an innocent heart and they preserve it, but if one is not born but with a black split heart, can one grow innocent by trying? It is not only of myself I am thinking, Uncle.

Uncle says that he does not accuse me of this, he says that the times are the times of a black split heart, with self-seeking driving a false-simple road for its own advantage through the bog and over the hearts. This was the false-simple way of the Nazis driving at the democracies, which are still too much split and dark, and on the defensive to preserve a way of life that shall encourage people to buy as many things as possible.

I say that when the war was on Basil Tait used to say that this Coal lord, Lord Rivaulx, was very dangerous, he had the power idea very strong. And what was he after, was it the Premiership? Yes, it was that, and it was the defeat of Russia, and the defeat of the idea to make life not safe for millionaires; and the defeat of the idea to make life without any cheap magazines and cinemas and washing-up machines, and football, and dogs, and fun fairs, yes, that is what he was against. That was the real war for Lord Rivaulx; yes, my word, that is where his Lordship is shooting straight. So he does not say openly: Let Russia go hang, but that is the idea he has. And all the time he was wishing to make peace with the Germans, for he does not understand one thing to understand it truly, for he has this illiterate cunning that told him he would be better off coming to terms with Germany, than with a sniff in the wind of a new idea coming out of Russia. Yes, my Lord, Basil says he is dangerous. But later, of course, he was not so dangerous because later he was put away under 18B, he was in Holloway. And now of course it is Russia that is so dangerous ... with the N.K.D.V., and Fear with his foot round the door. And the words that run with it ... the scientific use of force, pacification, re-education, exchange of populations, elimination of unreliable elements. Indeed, Uncle, I have heard our own Elks say that Truth is not absolute at all, but dialectical.

Uncle says he notices that I am fretful, but that this is not my nature, but that he supposes I have been associating with persons who expect an answer, and who think that in politics there is an answer.

144

There is no answer, he says: You would not expect an answer?

No, no, I say, feeling at once immensely lightened, I should not wish for an answer, and I smile at my Uncle and I say that I suppose an answer suffocates.

My uncle said that when he knew me when I was a child I was the happiest child.

Yes, yes, it will come back, I say, in a sulky cross voice. No, no, Uncle, I say, catching hold of his hand, I am not sulky.

I swing his hand slyly from side to side. Basil Tait is rather a fool, you know Uncle, I suppose it is him you were thinking I was associating with that wanted an answer, eh? He is like a fourteen-year-old clever boy, with his Lord Rivaulx and this and that. You would say: He is promising, he is like a fourteen-year-old boy you know, he thinks girls can't play. I begin to laugh. Uncle dear, I say, I suppose all the same you suppose there is an answer? and I suppose you suppose it goes like this, eh? It is a poem I wrote. You know, Uncle darling, my employer Lord Rackstraw at the Ministry, sometimes he takes me out for a treat, so one day he took me to hear a lecture by the great Dean Inge, that I admire so much, on Origen. He spoke wonderfully well, he had some wonderfully clear things to say, only unfortunately I think he was a little tired, or perhaps he did not think that the audience was quite up to it, because every now and then he would take a quick flip through the pages of his manuscript, letting ten pages flip by with never a word read. But first his sharp eyes would rake the rows where the people sat, and the eye would as much as say: No good, no good, no good, I'll keep the next ten pages for publication only, I'll have 'em for my book.

Dr. Inge, said my Uncle mildly, is a great man and a great scholar.

Yes, he is, he is. So I took one sentence that he said and out of that one sentence and the situation I made this poem:

Listen all of you, listen all of you,
This way wisdom lies
To reconcile with the simplicity of God
His contingent pluralities.

Oh, the wise man sat in his chair,
And oh, the people they would not hear,
They said: It is much too deep for us
As they turned to the Differential Calculus.

Oh, if the people had only heard
Him
Oh, if that wise man's word was not blurred
Not dimmed.

He was quoting Tertullian, said my Uncle.

We all have a very happy time this morning. Caz is smiling, and so is Tiny, and so am I.

Caz looks at me and says: A merry heart goes all the way, a sad heart tires in a mile-o. But he smiles too.

Yes, it is just that, it is the tiredness that makes us fret, it would be better to keep silent.

I think in the war Goebbel's propaganda made very good play with the tired and the sad, they began to think that Germany never made a mistake, that England always did; we should have been on our guard against this, better to keep silent.

In this the intellectual person is not always his country's best servant, he was not then and is not now. Yes, I think

146

a certain sort of intellectual person should always remember that the heart of the Germans was wrong, and the heart of their fight wrong, and that in their hearts they knew this, the Germans, and that this is the heart of their defeat. This sort of person I am thinking of should invert Christ's words, he should say: Remove first the beam from your brother's eye, and after that you can think about the mote in your own. For in the carping and the barking and the criticism there was a deadly poison that would strike the confidence from the English fighters, it would have done this.

When the commandos came back they were tired and dirty and happy men and they were greeted with cheers, the people lined up to cheer them. I wish I had been there. And they brought their willing prisoners with them and gave them their tea and cigarettes and blankets. That generosity in victory is something the Germans did not have, it is the better spirit.

In 1940, in June, when France fell and all the world backed us for surrender, there were perhaps three persons out of all England who would have sued for terms—not counting the aforesaid Lord Rivaulx, who was too open a villain to be dangerous—but there were perhaps three other men who were men of the highest intelligence, sitting aloft in the mandarin atmosphere of the higher intellect. Dessicated and remote, they knew history and had no sense in it; they knew their own country and their own people, and nothing of them; these men, with many a fine phrase, would have made terms with the Germans; they were these extremely intellectual persons, with the very highest or academic honours ... ah, ah, not to stretch for a gun, not to side with the gross Goering. To hell with Ingersoll that stirred these memories. No more of it.

XII

O<small>N SUNDAY MORNING</small> I go to church with Heber, and he preaches about taking no thought for the morrow, and Be not over-anxious. And it is this merry heart, he goes on to explain, and how it must be centred in God, for this merry heart has a holy lightness that has nothing to do with outside excitements, no, it is centred in God and happy, because it knows that not at all of itself can it be good, or be anything, but only in and through God.

Oh, this is a lightening flash of a thought, like the flash of a bright aeroplane in the sun, oh, one should hold it and seize it and hold to it, and not let the darkness come in again, that will be still darker for the light that has gone. So let me hold it, God, I pray.

In this long happy Sunday with Heber, working in the garden and helping Tuffie in the kitchen, it is like something that is soft and sure and sensible. But in London, in the London life it is not so easy. I wrote in my diary to-night about London:

> Cool and plain,
> Cool and plain,
> Was the message of love on the window-pane,
> Soft and quiet,
> Soft and quiet,
> It vanished away in the fogs of night.

To-day dawns sunny, and by nine o'clock it is already hot. My cousin and I are off for an excursion to the sea, once again we are riding together in a vista with distances; I have the pony Caramel, Caz rides old Noble, we are not nobly but adequately mounted.

We ride through the morning, slowly, lollingly; we take our feet out of the stirrups and dangle them in the long grass. We find the right place for lunch, and dismount and lie on the grass that is short turf on a cliff top. The place where we are now is drenched in sunlight, this sunshine has the quality of the eternal, it is absolutely classical. We are on a little promontary, where the low cliffs stand out a little way into the sea; the soft grass on top of the cliff is speckled with flowers, the flowers that my cousin will not let me pick.

Do you want to raise the devil? he says.

In the drenching beautiful sunshine, the pure light, it is like a dream. I stretch out my hand to touch my cousin; his skin is cool and firm, he is very much flesh and blood.

At once he says, I am the most flesh and blood of all your dream, and laughs again, that boring laughter that he has been laughing all the morning, that is getting on my nerves—The most flesh and blood. I turn over on my stomach and the scent of the beautiful grass placates me, so that, catching my cousin's mood, I laugh too.

The clean air, I say, the clean air, the beautiful soft grass, the grass against the soft stomach. I think I am like one of the Parnassians, dear Reader, do not ask me which one, who said that he was excited only by magnificent scenery. As the sunlight saturates my flesh and bones I feel I should like it to go on for a long time (comment disait Ingenuous Isabel dans le Pink 'Un d'autrefois). I shift myself, after a little while, to the edge of the cliff, and look down to where there are firm sands and a little staircase across the bay to the left of us.

Caz, dear, what a lovely *day*, what a lovely *bay*.

Casmilus sings gently. Presently he says: What are you doing? (I have been writing for some time.) Oh, writing letters, I say, writing letters to the dear ones I left.

Isn't it rather late? You will be seeing them soon.

No, I say, it is never too late, one must write when one is away, even if you post it at the station coming home. They will know you have written.

What have you written?

It is to Pearl and our Aunt, I say. Listen: I love you very much, more than anything else. I send you deepest dearest love. Adoringly, Sailor. That is for both of them. (I write and seal the envelope.)

Caz says: Why, 'Sailor'?

Because I left them, I say, I left them, I sailed away. Oh, Death.

Caz begins talking again; he does make me the most delightful impression of good companionship. I cannot stay angry with him for long.

I say: The sunlight is like the sunlight of Homer, it is eternal.

After a while I look at the flowers again. I say: 'Or that fair field of Enna, where Proserpine gathering flowers, Herself a fairer flower by gloomy Dis was gathered, Which cost Ceres all that pain.' I look aslant at Casmilus and see what I expect to see, the old-fashioned look I remember so well from childhood, the old-fashioned look slatting through his eyes.

Casmilus, I say, you need not look so furious, I dare not pluck the flowers. I fling myself into his arms. I say: It is not only the scenery, the dark sea and the laughterless stone,

150

I remember the other book where the shades must have blood to drink, where the dead cannot speak, they are so cold, they cannot speak, they cannot think, they have no memory unless they lap the warm blood.

Casmilus covers my face; the thought of the cold rivers of hell is fading from my mind.

I said to my cousin, on another occasion when we had gone horseback riding together: Do you like Death?

Caz said: He is nothing to write home about.

The wind blew then, and the sun shone, and the clouds came, and the shadows moved across the grass; the bay leaves burnt green in the Greek pool.

What is Death like? I said to my cousin, who had faced him, I supposed, many times.

I shouldn't know him from Adam, he said, and then he said again: He's nothing to write home about, and began to laugh.

Irritation at the vulgarity of my cousin's words prevailed upon a Grecian peace. I remembered so well the vulgarity of the phrases I used to the monstrous editor—'The nauseating necessity I have of writing to you,' and then I said: 'Can you not send me some money?' But the anger had been eating me up—Quis me vitupare audet, quod something, quod something else, quia audire nolim tam damnatos homines? I was become a Cicero of the grievance and the vulgar phrase.

At night time when one has a fever one thinks of the grief and the grievances. One will write a book then; ah, ah, ah, how thick the tears fall down. Page after page of the new novel unfolds itself. In the night hours, in the midnight hour of the flowers of revenge and memory, the novel is finished. It is called, My Humiliations. It needs but to add the title as the tears fall thick upon the burning flesh. Ah, ah, ah, My Humiliations.

I now begin to talk quickly. Sometimes at the Ministry, you know, Caz darling, I would sit in the lavatory, on the little chair by the washbasin, and I used to sit there and I used to look at the floor. It was a linoleum with a faint seagreen pattern. In one square there was a picture, it was a marbled pattern but it was a picture, if you looked at it sideways it was a picture, it was the picture of a noble owl swinging downstream; on a wide wing-span he swung down the track of the mountain stream, low down upon the roaring torrent. It was a Scottish mountain panorama, the stream and the banks were mottled with heather; it was Scotch-Baronial, period Balmoral-Vic. This owl had dark wide eyes, they were dark pools. It was a wonderful purposeful flight this owl had, with his dark shadowed eyes; there was no light in them at all, they were bottomless deep. Oh, I do not wish to think of the eyes of the dark owl, oh no, I do not wish to think of that; it is not the time. Oh, his eyes were so beautiful, Caz, you cannot imagine it.

I hurried on to say something trivial, something in a hurry, yet deliberate and cunning, to say something, it did not matter, any trivial thing at all, to stop the silence that was coming up from Caz and from the moment.

Did you know, Caz, that the atmosphere of the planet Jupiter is composed of equal parts of ammonia and marsh gas? How I should like to be there. (Oh no, that is not quite the note.)

I say: At the Ministry I was often sad, I wished to be alone, I wished that Rackstraw was not so often there, this kind old gentleman, this sweet Rackstraw, there was never so kind an old gentleman as Rackstraw. At the time just before Dunkirk he said:'Well, Miss Phose, it looks as if we should lose the B.E.F.' (with a heigh-ho and it can't be helped). He was a brave old man, he fought in the last war and was taken prisoner by the Turks. And now in this war, if he had been on the sands of Dunkirk, it would have been the same thing, himself on the terrible sands, with a heigh-ho and it can't be helped; we shall lose the B.E.F. I used to say to Rackstraw: 'You should go away, you should have a long holiday, you need a rest, you are looking tired, why don't you go away?' At the end he became sad: 'Can I not stay in my own office?' he said. Rackstraw was reading *The Life of Field-Marshal Lord Birdwood* and ticking off the people he knew. God bless the sweet boy, how quiet he is, how happy. It is curious, Caz, what beautiful things people will say in the everyday life. Harley used to say: 'We must break this cursed entanglement with Major Hamlet. . . .' And then he would say: 'I can touch my toes with my hands, I used to be so fat.' One day he came in with a lot of Christmas cards; he said: I've been had with these cards, I got them at Woolworth's; the top card is fine, those dogs are just right; I thought they were all the same, but look at this one, this dog is coming out of his kennel, his teeth are bared, it is called "Waiting for you". We'll have to be careful with that one.' And one day he said: 'What would I like to be if I could be anything I liked?—a financier.'

Caz now crept over the grass to where I was lying and took my hand away from the poppy stalks and began to press the finger tips backwards, singing to himself.

Also, I should like to have a bit of peace and quiet and a few acres in the country and a chicken farm.

What on earth for? said Caz.

No, that is what Harley says. And then he says: 'It looks like old G. will pull this business off; if so it means £20,000. I sometimes think he can't be all Jew, he's so damned unlucky; must have an Aryan grandmother.' And he said: 'I can't bear these cocktail parties, I went into the garden to be by myself for a bit, and then I went home.' That's what Harley says. And Rackstraw says: 'Did you happen to see those old ladies sitting by you at the *musicale* yesterday— Lady Weiber, Mrs. Van Rachet and Lady Blume? I looked at them, Miss Phoze, and I said to myself: "You're no beauty chorus. . . ."' And Rackstraw says: 'I wrote to the L.C.C., Miss Phoze. If they must pile the snow in heaps, I said, they need not do it in front of my front door'—the red carpet across the pavement, and the ladies, I suppose, may step in the puddle. And he says: 'There was a horrible little child at the week-end, I shouldn't care tuppence if I never saw him again. *The Times*, Miss Phoze,' he says, 'has never had a good word to say for Russia since the revolution; I took the matter up with them myself; I wrote to Segrave, I said: "Is your man telling the truth?"'

I now began to laugh so much that the tears rolled down my cheeks. But I grew serious. But, Caz, I said, there is another one at the Ministry, the third one, that St. John, that grave one that is the friend of Heber's, he does not like me in the way that Harley and Rackstraw do, he does not like me at all, he thinks that I tell Harley everything, he thinks that I am Spy Number One. He says: 'There goes the well-known spy, watch where she goes.' Often he will open the door of my room, and look in at me, and go away again; or, if my room is empty, if I am not there, he will open the door and he will look in, and I am not there, and he will cry: 'The cad is gone, where now is the cad running?'

I begin to cry: Oh, I am so sorry about this St. John, I say, because of all the high ones at the Ministry, it is he who has my respect. Oh, Caz, I am not a spy, indeed I am not this. But I say: If I am supposed to be a spy (and I grind my teeth and begin to look wicked) then a spy I will be with a vengeance.

Caz sinks his face on to my open hand: Oh, why do we cry; oh, why do we cry so much?

Oh, I don't know, everybody does, but some have not the courage to cry. It is the war, I say, and the war won, and the peace so far away. Some of our friends, I say, seek refuge in a high-pitched nervous giggle, very girlish. This goes on for a long time, it is no good, it is very facetious; very fatiguing for all of us, no good at all.

Life is like a railway station, said Caz, the train of birth brings us in, the train of death will carry us away, and meanwhile we are cooling our heels upon the platform and waiting for the connection, and stamping up and down the platform, and passing the time of day with the other people who are also waiting.

Yes, that is how it is. Of course for everybody it is not like this, for firmer types it is different.

Caz put his arm under my shoulder and made me sit up.

If you really want to die, he said, why don't you? He looked rather puzzled. But of course it is because you are romantic about death. Yes, he said, the train of death that you are waiting for is an excursion train, yes, that is what it is: All aboard for a day in the country.

He came up close against me and whispered in my ear: You must not be romantic about Tom, you must not suppose there is a solution there, there is no solution for us and no answer. Tom is a bad fellow.

He had spoken so low and so quickly, that it was as if nobody had spoken, as if the wind had blown.

He drew off from me and began to drawl in a rather loud voice. (This voice was as good as a wink, to pretend that he did not speak before, but his eyes do not draw off from me, his eyes say that it was he who spoke, and not the wind that blew; and not my thoughts that spoke, but his.)

Oh, he says now, I think it is this writing business that makes you so sad: Oh, it is that, on top of the war and after-the-war and being in the middle of things without the turning point yet come, that makes you cry. Oh, the writing business is very corrupting. (Caz looks away over my head, looking seriously.) Well, he says, look round at the writing people, what do you see, eh? You see greed, envy, self-righteousness, being puffed up, and vanity.

Yes, I said hurriedly, that is so. I went to a meeting once, a meeting of writers, and do you know, Caz, a person got up and said that writers were the leaders of the world, the influencers, the leaders, they were those to whom the people looked in their ignorance and distress, to whom they looked for guidance and a way out. Ha, ha, ha, ahem.

Yes, says Caz in this drawling voice, I find that remarkable, for they cannot rule themselves, so how can they rule others, to guide them and show them a way out? Why, look at So-and-so, he said (mentioning by name a certain agèd author, supposed to be great both as writer and influence, of a mandarin caste of mind, and a most noticeable bad conduct). There is a girl living with him, said Caz, and this girl submits to the most deplorable misbehaviour on the part of Snooks, she is both the victim of this misconduct and the condoner of it. But when one says: 'My dear Miss, how can you submit to those things, how can you bring yourself to it?' she says: 'I count it a privilege, not dearly bought, to live with this great Snooks and, through living with him, to meet, if only in a menial fashion, the great ones of this age. Why, these men are the Keats, the Shelleys, the Byrons, and the Tennysons of our days.' 'If you believe that, dear Miss,' I said, 'then you will believe anything.'

And he said that she should by all means read Snooks's poems, for there was in them much of value that a reader

156

might pull out, but that when he sought to teach, to pro-
nounce, to pontificate upon the moral plane, then let her
beware. There is much beauty in his writing, he said, that
may with profit be pulled out by the discriminating reader,
but his opinions, as moral judgments, as a way of life...?
A man's actions and his conduct are grounded in his thoughts,
and Snooks's actions and his conduct, being what they are,
of what value are his thoughts? But this little fool, he said,
would have none of it; the man Snooks was her idol, she
must swallow him whole, not only his unappetising ageing
person, but also his opinions and his philosophy. Writers'
books may, of course, hold useful matter, went on Caz
(of which the writer himself is not always fully conscious),
for all that the writers may be persons of low moral standing,
not to be associated with by the fastidious, scum of the earth,
indeed, of value only in their books, and only then by the
sifting process of the judging mind of the reader. So that
in one long book, said Caz, there may be only two thoughts
of beauty and of worth, and for these two thoughts the
reader must plunge and dive. The writer himself is to be
considered as a felon, put to hard labour in a solitary cell,
his work scanned by the warders, that are his readers,
scrutinized by them, and judged for what worth there
may be in it.

There is exaggeration in what you say, I said, but there is
truth in it, too, but there is in reality little need to take this
severe action against the writers. They are in a way the
scum of the earth, now too fêted, too set up, too beautified,
but I can assure you, Caz, if the writers like to think they
are persons of general influence and leadership, we need not
grudge them the pleasure they derive from this notion, for
there is in fact no substance in it; they are neither influencers
nor leaders, they are indeed wholly unattended to. Nor

can it be found, in the history of the whole world, that any writer has influenced the course of history, though by their written propaganda they may have advanced the causes already in existence which gained their approval and the use of their ready pens. Was Edward I a writer, who framed the laws of England, was Torquemada in his terrible zeal, was Wilberforce in his charity, was Nelson in his victories, was Newton, was Harley? Is the great scholar Coulton not foremost a churchman? The philosophers? you may object. But are they first and foremost properly to be considered as writers? The nonsense that I have heard spoken in certain quarters is not worth an answer. The answer is in the world that rolls before us.

Let them know where they stand, said Caz solemnly, and let them walk in humility, docile to their inspiration, dogged in its service. 'So to the measure of the light vouchsafed, shine Poet in thy place and be content.' In this way, and only in this way, may they attain to greatness. And when they have genius and are submissive to it, then indeed there is no saying where the spirit may not drive their poetry, their stories, their pictures, their sculpture. For this is the hard way of all the arts. If the artist chose the softer way of social or political prominence, his art suffers, he sins against it, he becomes indeed the scum of the earth. By the quality of their art they stand or fall, they are not otherwise to be considered.

How happy I felt now, lying beside my beloved wise cousin, my solemn friend. Why do I fret and cry because he can be nothing else than a friend? Was he not always my true friend, and is he not this now? It is sufficient to lie beside him in friendship and agreement. His thoughts and words run with mine.

Of course, I said, it is all very well to say the reader must be the judge, but we must remember that the reader is not always a person of the highest intelligence, we must be careful of that.

Care killed the cat, said Caz.

The foolish reader bites the man of genius.

The dog it was that died.

I laughed: I like best, Who bites the Pope dies of it.

We fell asleep in the sun.

When we woke up my cousin was again in his provocative mood, lazy, laughing, but questioning to get an answer from me.

Caz said: If you want to die so much, why don't you?

Oh, I don't know, Caz, really; one part of us wants to die, I suppose, and the other part does not, and the two are always crying out against each other, especially the part that does not want to die is crying always to be let off.

And the part that does not want to die, what does this part say, what has this part got to say for itself, eh?

Oh, well, it is something that it feels it has, something that it thinks is valuable, something that is an excuse from death. It is like the story of the girl who was married to a Caliph, she was a white girl, a beautiful white fat girl, she was going to have a baby. The neighbouring tribes were hostile, they broke in upon the Caliph's palace, and they murdered the Caliph and they murdered everybody, but then the beautiful white girl came out from the curtains, and she stood on the dais and she had only an indigo-blue silk cloak on, and she threw this back and she was naked, so she said, I bear under my heart the son of the Caliph.

And what did they do to her?

Oh, I don't know. They killed her, or they did not kill

her. It is always the same. Everybody feels this in the part of them that does not wish to die, so they begin to cry, and they cry out, 'I carry under my heart the son of the Caliph'. I think in the story they cut him out, this son of the Caliph, so he was born without blemish by a Cæsarian section.

You are very fond of Lopez, aren't you? said Caz. He picked some poppies now and was splitting the stalks and threading them to make a chain.

Yes, oh yes. I love the friendship with the friendly girls. Of course, yes.

Caz is mad about death this morning. He says: Would you like to see Lopez at a further reflection?

In the darkness, I say, in the darkness by the lake of quick-silver? No; if I must, later. But now I do not wish to see her like this.

You think of death as a sleep and the end of it. It might be a series of reflections, like the mirrors that are set up against each other.

I love the friends and the friendships, I say, and by and by even my friend Eleanor will come back to me.

My cousin looks at me with an enigmatic smile. I see you are really very happy, he says, quite at home.

There is nothing to say now for a little while; we lie and stare at each other. I should like to speak to my laughing cousin. Tentatively, tenderly, in a child's measure, I should like to say to Casmilus, I am perfectly happy, I am in love with my life. But there is fog and mist in my throat and a little snoring noise. I cannot say it, I *love*, and, imperiously, you *must*. To love—as a verb that is not transitive? How can one say such a thing? My hand curls inside his fingers, I hide my head.

Casmilus begins to sing, he sings in a soft drawling voice, a soft winning drawl, the words are nonsense, something from a grammar book, de chez l'Institut Français. Casmilus sings: *Moi, c'est moralement que j'ai mes élégances, je ne m'attife pas ainsi qu'un fréluquet. Mais je serais plus soigné si j'étais moins coquet.*

It is for myself I am singing that, he says, with an exaggerated polite air, I sing it thinking *only* of myself. You understand?

Oh, yes. I do not wish to cough and drawl into the darkness, I say, I think that death is certainly very near; at this moment death is near to us, and yet it is also nothing at all. For if death is what we are not, how can we have a part in it? When we become death, how can we fear and hate and love? But we can do all these things very sturdily now, and are superior to death. I say to Casmilus, I have written a poem that is a farewell present for you and for Heber, something for you to have. I say the poem:

> I have two friends,
> There are two friends of mine.
> One is my father,
> And one my Divine,
> My father stands on my right hand
> He has an abstracted look
> Over my left shoulder
> My Divine reads me like a book.
> Which shall I follow,
> And following die?
> No longer count on me
> But to say good-bye.
>
> Á leur insu
> Je suis venue
> Faire mes adieux
> Adieu, adieu, adieu.

161

This poem makes such a terrible picture of a terrible state of mind, like the poet when he wrote: Go thou, poor child of woe, that I fall to tears of burning pity for all who are in this condition, that is for everybody that I know; yes, nobody at all at this moment does not seem to me to be in this state.

If I never see you again, Casmilus darling, I say, after you have gone I mean, I want you to know. . . .

I lean back hard against him and begin to laugh, for the contradictory nature of the idea of this phrase—for if one is dead, does it matter?—I want you to know. . . .

Well, what do you want me to know? says my cousin, who has now thrown his posy chain into the cornfield.

That . . . I laugh so much that I can hardly speak, and already I am so extremely tired. . . .

Well?

That you will never forget me.

He began to laugh again at this, and he held me in his arms, and a little way off the great oak branches stirred in the wind that was now blowing up strong, and the sound of the leaves in the wind seemed to echo his laugh, and make a sense of their own that was no echo, or if it was an echo it was one from far away, that spoke to me in German, in a long forgotten voice that was half-sneer and wholly base, *Hast Du dich verirrt?*

How curious fear is when it runs in the mind. At the Ministry once I was looking at a magazine, it was a cheap girls' paper, there was upon the cover the figure of a hooded monk with a crookt hand stretching out, and a finger in silhouette. 'Oh,' I said to Harley, 'that is frightening, yes, that is very good, yes, if I saw that I should be frightened.' 'Yes,' he said, 'it is frightening.' Then he said, 'That dead lilac you have on your mantelpiece reminds me of somebody.' 'Florrie Silbermann,' I said.

What are you frightened of, Celia? said Caz, and then he laughed. I never knew a man, he said, who believed that death was the end of it, their hopes might be set on mortality, but always there was the fear that indeed death might not be the end. But now he spoke more gently: You are afraid of the torturers of this world, he said, you wish to be on the edge, to stay a little and then go, but in this going there is this hope that something may come up that is beautiful scenery and a country day. You are waiting on the platform with friends, for the excursion train.

It is love that everybody is after, make no mistake, I said, 'Here is no home'.

But everything that I had been saying at once collapsed, it was as if it had never been, it was nothing.

You flee the torturers, said Caz, with another nasty laugh, and then he said: She flees, but none pursues.

At these words I am already in a desert of snow, there are no footsteps and the sky is a shutter.

Oh, yes, I cry. You, Caz, you pursue, you pursue to the death. Caz, I say, I once saw you, you were standing on the bank of a stream at the other side. There was a man with you, he had a plaster caste of a baroque face, with an elegant long nose, a little chipped. So there he stood, this plaster baroque person, and he twirled an hourglass at the end of a black moiré ribbon.

I never stood with such a companion, said Caz.

Oh, yes you did. I was walking by this stream and then standing still. It was a February filldyke ditch, flowing dirty below a factory town; very grim it was, this stream, and the factory town that could never be a city.

So what happened? said Caz.

Oh, I slipped, I fell; I fell into the stream.

And I fished you out, I suppose?

No, you did not move. And they said: 'That will shift her,' for they were tired of my long death song. That will shift her, and I struck my head on an underwater snag. 'That will shift her,' they said; that indeed did.

It was a dream, said Caz.

No, no. Dreams are about shoes standing in shallow bathwater.

I remember that once, many years ago, it was before the war, my cousin and I were staying in a foreign town. Casmilus used to take me to the old church of St. Stephen. This, and the large graveyard surrounding it, were oddly placed—but a few steps from the Jewish quarter of the town, where the poor Jews had their houses. The first day we were there the snow fell softly, but it did not lie on the ground for long because the April thaws was come, it was March and the cold winter was nearly passed. The grave-yard was brown and white and frog-green, overhung by a yellow mist, infinitely mournful. Wrapped in my over-coat and with rubber overboots upon my feet, I walked beside my cousin. Walking beside him, silent in the smudgy snow, I feel more of a niece to him than a cousin. He is tall, he does not speak. I feel solitary and reconciled to solitude, as face to face once for all with the infant heart, and locked with it fast, past hope of growth. I stand in the foreign grave yard and stretch my arms against a tombstone, that records the death of Thomin Krak, his business in life, his gifts to charities, his many dutiful sons and daughters, and so speaks last of all of Elizabeth his wife. But it is only to say: 'And of his wife Elizabeth.' And I think of the other wife who was about to die, who thought of her young son, and with no irony at all of her important late husband, and so she said to her attendant, *Parles-lui tous les jours, des virtus de son père, et quelquefois aussi, parles-lui de sa mère. . . .* 'And of his wife Elizabeth.' But, stretched against the tombstone, I wanted to pray, but the literary thought cut devilishly deep and split the thoughts. 'Our father, our father,' but what is it that then comes? Casmilus was looking at me with a dark expression. I shouted to him then: Casmilus, I am a child of Europe, Christianity is the religion of Europe, you have become contaminated by Buddhist thought in an Eastern passage, but for a European it is fadism, it is to make nonsense of it.

Oh, yes, of course, he said: Christianity is the religion of Europe.

I turned away from him and prayed in a gabble: Thou art all that we know of good and very much more, Thou art all wisdom, truth and beauty, Thou art love, Thou art the source of our being and the desire of our hearts, grant that we may return again to Thee.

Casmilus came at me then very direct: You feel very close to death here? he said.

Because it is so cold? Yes, it is cold, and sad.

And Christian, eh?

I said: It might be the sheeted dead, they thought that it was very cold and longed for blood, that they might lap it up and take again for five minutes the hue and substance of life.

Caz said: That idea of death is not entirely Christian, there is little thought there for sin and retribution, vicarious atonement and salvation.

Nor is it not entirely pagan either, I said, nor wholly held among them. Lucretius wrote to free them of it: all was nothing, he said, remembering the alternative, the sheeted shadows gibbering for a joke in the plays of Aristophanes, but so sad and cold . . . 'where death is we cannot be, and where we are, death is not'.

I began to turn and scream, screaming out loud against the tombs and the snow. Caz took me away then. The Christian child, he said, and laughed out loud, and pulled me away from the carved headstone . . . the European Christian child. We went off then to find some hot soup and some wine.

It was ten years ago, it is to-day. My cousin is lying beside me on the summer grass. My cousin is lying on his back, I am stretched out beside him with the poppies at my head. The sun sucks the drowsy smell out of the poppies, the wind has dropped, there is not a cloud in the sky; the bees drone round.

We sleep till four o'clock by British Double Summer Time, that is two o'clock by the sun. When we wake up we are in a more practical mood. It is wonderful to wake up strong in the early afternoon hot sunshine at four o'clock. Just the time for a swim, says Caz.

We go down the cliff, down the hard mud-baked path beside which the feathery plants grow high; the mud is hardbaked and cracked beneath our bare feet, when we get to the esplanade it is made of hot white stone that is smooth like marble. In the middle of the white road that crosses the esplanade there is a baby crawling fiercely. How reckless the creature is, I pick him up, he is very heavy, his hair is bleached white by the sun, his romper suit bulges over his fat back. He begins to roar and stiffen. As he cries out a tall thin pale girl comes running out of the shelter. 'Oh, he is so naughty,' she says, 'I can never leave him for a moment, I must have fallen asleep.' Well, there is not much traffic about, I said, looking at the empty miles before us and behind. How swiftly he crawls, he is bold and forceful.

The mother sighs and takes him from me. The child has sucked the strength quite out of her, she is pale and shadowy, he is a lion in the road. She carries him down the slipway on to the sandy beach and sits down in the shadow of the breakwater, the child sprawls across her knees, at once he is asleep, the girl also is asleep, a little crab crawls over her ankles. There is a rich strong smell of iodine that comes from the tide-washed black baked seaweed that hangs against the breakwater.

We walk along the beach for some way, up and down the ribbed sand hummocks, jumping the breakwaters, but sometimes there is a great difference in the sand levels on either side of the breakwaters. Then we stand on the wooden crossbeams and jump from a height to the sand upon the other side. In the deep pool by the breakwater there are starfishes, there is a whorl in the sand where a crab burrows.

We came at last to a low stone causeway jutting far out into the shallow sea. If we walk to the end of this, said Caz, we may be able to get a dive, otherwise we shall have to paddle half across to Germany.

We walk swiftly along the marble mole, as we go further and further from the land we see that the paving stones of the causeway are broken; the sea swings calm but very strong.

It is an earthquake sea, says Caz, looking at the strange light from the depths of the sea and the strong swinging movement. Take care you do not slip.

At the end of the mole there is an inverted lobster pot on a pole.

It is a wonderful smell of fish out here, I say, it is an especially English smell of an English washed coast, the *English* fine days are so much better than the others because of the wet days that go before and come after; so to-day is clean and washed bright, and to-morrow will be wet again.

To-day it has been baked for a long time, said Caz, it is unearthly hot and still.

I lie on my back on the hot white stones and let my fingers dangle in the sea. It is earthquake weather, I said, make no doubt.

It was earthquake weather in India once, said Caz, and the snakes came swimming out from the land.

The snakes that swim are always poisonous, I said.

Only if they are really sea snakes, said Caz, these were landsnakes that were taking to the sea to get away from the earthquake.

It was earthquake weather at Hythe once, I said (to change the conversation away from snakes), and all the dead sea fish came up from the deep bed of the ocean, and they floated in upon the steep shingle beach, as it is in those parts, and their stomachs were split quite open, and the smell of the dead fish girdled the coast from Dungeness to Shakespeare's Cliff, and may be right round the coast to Sandwich and Deal, and the smell of it came up inland for a matter of a mile or so, you could catch the whiff of it coming in by car from Ashford.

I can't help thinking Canterbury would be better, said Caz.

I took the cold damp seaweed in my hand and squeezed it tight. Now let us dive.

Caz got up and dived. I could see his body under the sea at a great depth. I stood up and did a surface dive. We went for a long quiet swim. I could not keep up with Caz, but swam quiet and melancholy in his wake. There was no cross-tug from the current, but a steep rise and fall of the whole sea, as if it was a person taking deep breaths so as not to become angry. We swam straight out towards the skyline. Swimming feeble breast stroke, low down in the water like a dog, I followed my strong swimming cousin; the light that the sun struck off the water was dazzling. I put my face against the sea and opened my eyes in the strong salt water, the sun beating down through the water was hot against my shoulders, far down I could see the wrinkled brown sand and sometimes a waving ribbon of shining brown seaweed. We were now swimming above a sandbank some half mile or so from the mole. Presently the sandbank broke surface and we climbed out and stood up on it. All around us was nothing but the sea and the sand and the hot still air.

Look, I said, what is this coming? (It was a piece of wreckage that was turning round and round in the current by the sandbank and coming towards us.) Why, I said, it is a cat. And there sure enough standing spitting upon the wooden spar was a young cat.

We must get it in, said Caz, and stretched out to get it.

But I saw that the cat was not spitting for the thought of its plight—so far from land, so likely to be drowned—but for a large sea beetle that was marooned upon the spar with the cat, and that the cat was stalking and spitting at. First it backed from the beetle with its body arched and its tail stiff, then, lowering its belly to the spar, it crawled slowly towards the beetle, placing its paws carefully and with the claws well out.

Why look, said Caz, its jaws are chattering.

The clatter of the teeth of the hunting cat could now be heard as the spar came swinging in to the sandbank. Caz made a grab for the spar, but the young cat, its eyes dark with anger, pounced upon his hand and tore it right across. Caz let go with a start and the piece of wreckage swung off at right angles and was already far away upon the current.

We could not have taken it with us, I said, while Caz dabbled his hand in the water to get the blood off. That cat is fighting mad, it does not wish to be rescued, it is, I said, very much like Lopez's cat Eto to look at, the same baleful eyes and the same angry teeth chattering at the hunt; it is no good, he is gone. Lopez's cat, I said, is a sombre cat, it will never play with her, though she will play with it all day, coaxing it and waiting upon it with fish and milk.

Clearly an animal without a heart, said Caz, and began to stand up in the middle of the sandbank in the hot still air and to perform the hornpipe, because he said that in spite of the hot air he was becoming chilled. As he danced the hornpipe in the sea deserts, with nothing to be seen but the sea rolling all around us, so I thought might the British mariner have danced in the midday light upon a desert rock in the slow swinging Pacific, the abandoned shipwrecked British sailor with his skilful twinkling feet, and his waxed pigtail a-fly behind him, as he danced so solemn-like to the porpoises and the mermaids, under the lonely tropic sun.

I clapped my hands in time to the hornpipe. Quicker, quicker, quicker danced my cousin, until at length he fell breathless into the ocean and struck out for home.

Back, he cried to me over his shoulder, back, the wind is getting up.

There was, as a matter of fact, no wind getting up, and no stirring at all in the still air, but underneath us as we swam the sea heaved more strongly than before. It is the core of the earthquake, I said, it is moving strongly.

When we got back we were cold after being in the water so long. We dressed quickly and went in search of tea, and were so lucky as to find one teashop that was empty and open and willing to serve us.

Where is the girl and her baby? I said, for the tide was now flowing swiftly over the flat beach.

We sat on the empty terrace beneath a bright torn awning. There was no sign of them, and no sound to be heard except the squawking of the seagulls fishing the shallows.

On the terrace it was desolate, remote, warm and sunny. I said: This is the best day of the holiday, the best, the longest.

Caz began to talk to me about the mountains of China, where he had been on an intelligence passage. There was the rain, he said, and the wind and the sparse spruce trees and the snowline, and then the emptiness and the king blizzard, and all the time there was the little pushing ponies of Tibet, and no people but the bearers, no loving friends, no people at all.

Caz spoke in the most soft monotonous winning tones, my heart and the thoughts went out to the Chinese distances.

Oh, Caz, I said, take me away, let me come with you, let me come with you on my pony, let me go away.

Oh, yes, said Caz, and what about the caliph and his son, eh, what about that? And to wander purposeless is to be a ghost, I do not wander purposeless, or for failure or escape, I wander under commission, I have my commission, to do this and that, with a purpose and within a time.

I looked at him in his eyes, it was the dark eyes of the flying owl.

Caz, I cried, Caz, I wish to come with you. I have no son of the caliph under my heart, I wish to come.

My teacup fell from my hand and I began to cry and scream, for there was such a pain in my heart as twisted my heart and muscles, so that I was bent backwards as though it was an overdose of strychnine.

171

Caz took me on his knees. I lay head down with my face to the sky, bent backward across his knees. I saw the blue afternoon sky through the delicate iron palings of the sea restaurant upside down. I looked through the wrought iron pattern and through the iron work to the blue sky, and downward to the dark blue sea that was indigo blue at the horizon.

It was for the pain in my heart that I cried, and for the bitter thought of the words I had said and the failure. The dark eyes of the flying owl was like a curtain to draw one behind it. I fell asleep. When I woke up I was riding again in front of my cousin, leaning back against him as we rode together on the old horse Noble. We led Caramel on a string.

XIII

AT SUPPERTIME to-night Tuffie was crying into the vegetables and the soup because she had anxious news of her daughter Dinah serving with the A.T.S. in Palestine, and Tiny was crying thinking of his brother, and Caz was frozen silent, and Uncle Heber was sitting quietly at his end of the table, and I was crying for the wickedness in my heart, and for the hopeful feeling of refreshment that now it should soon be over, now washed quite away. So there we sat, all of us, in silence and truth, and to be washed quite away. And I saw the evening paper lying by my plate, and the paragraph about a divorce case that had not succeeded, and the judge said that he sympathized with the plaintiff, but that inability to institute or to sustain a conversation was no grounds for divorce.

I pushed the cold mutton pie away from me and put my head on my arms on the table. Why had I railed against people to make them speak? If they did not wish to speak, why should they speak?

The semolina pudding came in on the trolly. I served a portion to Tiny and I said: Tiny, be sure that Clem will come, but do not think of Clem, think of Vera. For, I said, if you cry for fear you are an abject character.

Heber said that he agreed; he said that it was better to cry for love than for fear, but best of all for repentance.

I went up to Heber where he was sitting, and took hold of his hand.

One must be practical, Uncle, I said, it is necessary to be sensible. Look, I said, showing him a poem I had written that had just come by post at proof stage for publication. This poem is not sensible, it is, perhaps you will say, morally indefensible. Listen (I read the poem):

> I married the Earl of Egremont
> I never saw him by day
> I had him in bed at night
> And cuddled him tight.
>
> We had two boys, twins,
> Tommy and Roly,
> Roly was so fat
> We called him Roly-Poly.

(I began to sigh more deeply as I read on in my poem, for the hopelessness of the situation and the lack of what is sensible.)

> Oh, that was a romantic time,
> The castle had such a lonely look,
> The estate,
> Heavy with cockle and spurge,
> Lay desolate.
>
> The ocean waves
> Lapped in the castle caves.
>
> Oh, I love the ramshackle castle,
> And the room
> Where our sons were born.

Oh I love the wild
Parkland, the mild
Sunshine.

Underneath the wall
Sleeps our pet toad,
There the hollyhocks grow tall.

My children never saw their father,
Do not know
He sleeps in my arms each night
Till cockcrow.

Oh I love the ramshackle castle
And the turret room
Where our sons were born.

That is not sensible, I said, it is not sensible.

I often feel quite lost, too, said Caz hurriedly, and he put his hand over his eyes.

Oh, speak to us, Uncle, speak to us, I said. But why should I make him speak, if he does not want to speak, why should he speak?

My Uncle raised his eyes and looked at Caz and me with a look that was sorrowful and firm.

The poem is quite pretty, Celia, he said. I do not know whether it is sensible or not.

What do you mean by sensible? said Caz. He took his hands from his face and slapped them down on the table.

I mean what the great Churchill said, that overall directive that came through from the Very Important Person, from Cabinet level, from the great Churchill himself. It was at the time we were vilely engaged with the vile French

Admiral. 'Kiss Darlan's so-and-so,' roared the great Churchill, 'but get the French fleet.'

Tiny now left the room with his pocket handkerchief pressed to his face.

Caz laughed. Yes, that is sensible, that is really the whole of the English common sense. The French seeking *La Gloire* find infamy, the English seeking victory find glory.

Caz walked round the table and put his arms round me. The poem is a fairy story, he said, it is fanciful. The English, he said, are fanciful, as they are also sensible; there are the two English animals, you know; always against the Lion of commonsense there stands the Unicorn of fancy. This is not my own idea, he said; as a matter of fact, I found it the other day when I was reading that Indian chap, the poet, critic, or something, I can't remember his name.

After supper we had the very great relief of listening to *Maud* being read on the radio by Robert Harris; he read for three-quarters of an hour; his voice was controlled, strong, clear and sensitive, never strained, never affected. I thought: So there goes our hero to the Crimean War for his *seelische Entlassung*, and no thought for him whether it was a good war, or the right war, or the right front, et cetera. So off he goes, as happy as the day is long, to fetch a bullet in a simple death. And I thought: Here indeed is the great Tennyson a-roar, God bless the great Tennyson. And God blessed him and he wrote: 'A still small voice said unto me, Thou art so full of misery, Were it not better not to be? Then to the still small voice I said, I cannot cast into the grave, what is so wonderfully made.' Hurra.

And what did Tennyson say when the reader bit at him, when the sheep-like shallow-pate of a reading public ventured a word of protest, 'A word in your ear, if I may make so bold'—if they *dared* demur? What the great

Tennyson, the supposedly meek and mild Old Blether of
a Queen's pet baa-lamb, said was this:

> Vex not thou the poet's mind
> With thy shallow wit
> Vex not thou the poet's mind
> For thou canst not fathom it.

Hurra three times.

So I came up to my bedroom with my head full of *Maud*,
and full, too, of the thoughts of our modern love stories
that are never, oh, never right, but also are never wrong
in the simple noble way of going wrong that Tennyson has
in his great poem.

So to rid myself of the spell of *Maud*, and of the temptation
to proceed with Maud to still further lengths of not being
sensible, I drew from my wardrobe the old manuscript of
a short story I wrote some years ago, that was the love story
of two friends of mine. It is called *Over-Dew*, for that is the
name of the house my friend Cynthia told me, at least it is
near enough—too near by half you might say. So here is
the story.

OVER-DEW

This became a dread name for Cynthia in 1937. It was then
that Mr. Minnim first began to talk openly about his dear
wish. How dear it was to be for all of them.

Mr. and Mrs. Minnim had two sons who had done well
at school and won scholarships to Oxford. Their boyhood
was a happy time for all. Then the eldest son married Helen,
a fellow student at the university, and coming down found
a good post with sufficient money. His wife also had money
of her own; they were doing well.

The younger son Georgie was engaged to Cynthia, but

that did not go so well. He took a first in Greats, but then the difficulties began; he could not find a job. He did nothing, tried again, no good. He grew sulky. It seemed hopeless.

It was now that the dread name of *Over-Dew* was spoken and a scheme bruited. It was this. The Minnims were sincere and practising Christians; to Mr. Minnim anyone who was not a Christian was a half-educated person. It was for instance suggested that his daughter-in-law should write a life of St. Benedict. There was no good life of St. Benedict, said Mr. Minnim. So Cynthia suggested that Helen should write it, because Helen was a medieval history student, whereas Cynthia herself was a Latinist. So why not Helen, with her special knowledge? But Helen was not a 'Christian'. So: No, said Mr. Minnim, she was a half-educated person.

The *Over-Dew* idea was orthodox Christian. When Mr. Minnim retired from his accountancy work he said that they should move from the suburb where they lived and buy the house of *Over-Dew*, which was a retreat for missionaries to have on their leave holidays in England. But now it was being run, he said, in a fantastical fashion. When they bought it everything would be different, and better. Where was the money to come from? No matter. They had their savings, also they had the faith of Mr. and Mrs. Minnim. Mrs. Minnim loved her husband and was proud of him and pleased to follow him to the end of the world. And certainly *Over-Dew* was not that.

But, oh, when Cynthia heard that word it was the knell to all her life and love. This, she said, is the end of happy days and the beginning of calamity. *Over-Dew*, she thought, shall be the death of my love, and the death of life. For to that tune, she thought, shall come up a European war and personal defeat.

The Georgie situation was already sad. What could she do there? Nothing, but to see him and be silent, and so enrage. Or see him and speak, and the more enrage. The wise and affectionate Cynthia must break the engagement and give back the ring. There is nothing but this that she can do. She takes up a post at another university and in lecturing and study passes the days, no more of that. She has read a paper to her pupils and fellow-dons; the subject is the development of Latin from the first early growth upon the Grecian models. The study entrances; she finds and reads a Latin prayer: *I devote to Hades and Destruction*. It is a prayer for time of battle, the thought is this: I dedicate the enemy to Hades and Destruction. And perhaps one or two of the praying Romans will devote also themselves to Hades and Destruction. Rushing then into battle, these 'devoted' people hope they may be killed. If not, they are held for dead; they are stateless and in religion have no part at all. The gods have not accepted them; they are alive, but yet they are destroyed.

In Cynthia's life this sad year was twice as long as all the happy years before. She must now withdraw from Georgie, and see him miserable. She is at work and fast within her family, the happy careless laughter of the brothers and sisters rings her round. She has the home tasks too; and thinks of Georgie.

At the end of the year, in the bitter cold snow that fell that Christmas, the phrenzied Minnims moved from their life-long suburb.

The house of *Over-Dew* lay buried half in snow; it stood five miles from any town, upon a hillside. Very bleak it was, and all the pipes were froze. Mrs. Minnim worked hard, they had a girl to help them; then she left. Mrs. Minnim had courage and she was cheerful, but she was by

179

now an old lady. Suddenly there was the gift of a little money. Mr. Minnim bought chasubles for visiting priests. But at first there were no visitors at all, but only the old cold house, and the lavatories frozen up, and wood kindling to be chopped and dried. The work was bitter hard. Mr. Minnim, released suddenly from the routine of accountancy, suffered in his head a strange numbness. He moved about in a dream, would take no hand with the dishes. Even when five-and-twenty missionaries came for a conference, he would do nothing. He paced the garden plots . . . 'and here,' he said, 'I will build twelve new lavatories. . . . And in this room we will have a consecration and build an altar.'

The thaw came and turned all to mud and slush. There was still no post for Georgie. He came down from Oxford and washed the dishes for his mother, and chopped the wood, and moved also in a daze. The immense learning lay off from him; the crude work of the house was an excuse from study.

But now Mrs. Minnim was not happy. Like a sad animal she roamed the rooms of *Over-Dew*. This woman, who had been so boisterous and so loving, with many friends, but still her own best thoughts for Mr. Minnim and their sons, was like a sad animal that cannot know a reason.

Georgie, with the guilt of the excuse upon his heart, grew savage with her. The moody silences were shot with cruel words. It was so bitter cold within that house, though now without the snow was melted and turned to slush.

The money situation preyed upon the mind of Mrs. Minnim, but her husband spoke of faith. In the suburb where they had lived the friends said: 'How are the Minnims? Did you hear that Mr. Minnim had bought chasubles?' And then the foolish unkind laughter. 'Chasubles! It will be the ruin of them, the end.'

There was one hope that Mrs. Minnim had; it was this. That they might return at last to their house in the suburb. She had refused to let her husband sell this house. No, that must be for a return. No, that she would not allow. But now out of this refusal was made the bitterness of their life at *Over-Dew*. 'For,' said her husband, 'you kept back the seven hundred and fifty pounds; we might have sold the house for seven hundred and fifty pounds.'

In London the girl who should have been Georgie's wife hears all and understands, loves George, is helpless, reads to her class the Latin prayer: *I devote to Hades and Destruction*. She rules the harsh thoughts that run, cries: Come, love of God.

When I had finished this, I read it through and began to sigh, it was so sad, but not like *Maud* is sad, oh not like *Maud* at all; for *Maud* is wild, and this is nervous.

I hear the clock strike downstairs. It is now eleven o'clock. So, Georgie, I think, is now in Burma, and Cynthia has her work and is in London, and still they torment each other by airgraph, that can neither quit nor agree. So my tears fall slow for the ridiculous picture of mama and papa and the boys and girls jigging up and down in a nervous situation that is eternally ridiculous and eternally unbearable; and is my situation and is Caz's.

Tennyson gave his creatures dignity in suffering; he did not think them absurd, but we do, yes, in our heart of hearts we think that the *Maud* situation is very absurd indeed, for the life that we know does not, oh does not give dignity in suffering, indeed the life that we know seems like the Nazis to give always the maximum of pain with the maximum of indignity. So we cannot believe a word of the *Maud* situation. O.K., Maud, I thought, come into your

Sir-John-Millais garden, and stand by the Sir-John-Millais lilies with your blue-eyed lover, you doll-faced fib, you beauty. We know all about it, Arthur Hughes. So I thought after all there might be truth in my story and the sap of strife and life.

I go along to my cousin's room to listen to the News. ... A Dakota has crashed in Switzerland; the Judge has summed up in the Boiler Case ('No English wife is required to submit to such behaviour'); a tug has been lost with all hands off the Mumbles; the mallard duck on the top of Canada House has at last hatched out her chickens; a bottle containing luminal tablets ('dangerous to children') has been lost in Church Street, Kensington; 5,000 people are now known to have lost their lives in the Bengal Hindoo-Moslem riots. The Pope is better.

Caz, I said, are you off to-morrow?

Yes.

The room was full of the litter of departure, kitbags already spilling over that would surely never shut, empty bottles, service clothes, shaving tackle, belts, a revolver with its leather holster lying beside it, a pile of old books in the corner, torn letters in the waste paper basket.

I don't feel I can do any more to-night, said Caz. Let's go out for a bit. Where's Tiny?

He's in his room, I think. I heard some soft sobs as I came past.

My, oh my, said Caz, in his irritating off-American accent. He certainly does seem to have got that brother of his on the brain. I shouldn't be surprised if he turned up after all.

Oh, Caz, you don't really think Clem will come, do you?

Shouldn't be surprised.

We got our coats and went out by the side door. It was

182

a stormy night, with the clouds racing across the moon and the black shadows down by the spinney. Caz took my arm and we went under the branches towards the river.

This is *Maud* if you like, he said, this is old *Maud* with a vengeance.

Yes, I said, it lies in the scenery, oh what an elegant midnight pastorale; that is what is wrong with my story, there is no scenery in it.

I shivered and began to draw away.

Don't go yet, Celia, stay a little.

He stooped quickly and kissed me, he was looking down at me and smiling.

Do not be so sad, Celia, do not be sad.

The delight of the dream is in the scenery, I said, the smiling bright night has the appearance of peace, it is a smiling dream, oh how sinister is the dream that wears a smile.

Men pray for peace, said Caz, but when it comes they are like rabbits that foul their pasture, like dogs they lift their legs upon it and say: 'Peace hath her victories no less than war, but no one quite remembers what they are.'

I laughed. I said: I love that, Caz, I love it, but men are noble animals; they are not dogs and rabbits. 'Ay, Mother, mother, what is this Man, thy Darling kissed and cuffed, thou lustingly engenderst, to sweat and make his brag and rot, crowned with all honour and all shamefulness.'

I shifted in his arms, frowning slightly.

Don't go yet, Celia, don't scowl.

It was better, I said, in the war. Now it is flat, and the heart has gone out of it, and there is no fighting now on the grand scale, but only the deadly puzzling post-war skirmishing, the flatness of Occupation, the sullen German people, the unreasonable Jews. The victors, at war with the aftermath of war, grow tarnished, they are restless, they long for home, which way shall they look? The thoughts split up and the will slackens; in Germany only the cigarettes are profitable. In the war, in the years of defeat, in the blackest years, we used to say: It will be better when we swing into the offensive. Something is coming out of Africa, I said then, mark my words. You know, Caz, there is something devilish about war, devilish exciting I mean. 'Earth hath not anything to show more fair,' ahem, it is different now, is it not?

I leant over the palings of the little bridge, my eyes close upon the dark water. An army, I said, in victory, full tongue across the desert 'For pleasure and profit together allow me the hunting of men'. It is exciting, is it not? And it is masculine. I sighed again. But here we are, caught in the bewilderment of a post-war consequence, the trivial, the boring, the necessary, the inescapable; what is one's duty.

Caz pulled me back from the rotting handrail and I turned and looked at him. Fortunate face, I thought, departing and alert. There was the English general, I said that stood on the mound when the Germans broke in 1918, he looked at them through his field-glasses, he looked at them close, at the men lying piled up and tired, kaput, fed oop. So he looked at the Germans and he said, I think they're beat. There's the masculine thing in that, I said laughing, *Es ist ausgeziechnet*. Or whatever it is.

Caz laughed. I wish I could take you with me, he said, it would be just the life for you, I can see that now, you would enjoy it.

You will be in Delhi the day after to-morrow?

Yes, I am flying out in a bomber. I expect I shall sleep in one of the bomb racks.

Sleep well.

184

I looked down at the running water, the black water, at the white full moon afloat in midstream, the round dead face, the pale face. I put on a voice that is rather peculiar, familiar, too, rather lisping and thin, it squeaks a little at a high pitch. Caz, I say, listen. And in this put-on voice I say, 'You are quite potty about death, how do you go on about death, listen if she can think of one other thing—death, death, death. I see you with black sequins and seaweed clinging to your hair. You are like the child in the story who saw the Italian funeral, very grand it was, and as black as a maidservant's dream of death, and the child cried out, *Che gusto avrei di morir' anch' io*. You, my dear, might have been that little Roman, oh dear, oh dear, the little Roman monster amorous of death, of a maidservant's dream of death, be-jetted, be-feathered, be-sequined, death, death, death.'

Caz, I said, that is Clem, that is what Clem said to me, gibing in a flirt of bad temper, that is himself responsive only to the pomps of life, the Marquess of Carrabas and the sly puss.

Caz now led me away and we went off together, treading the dark forest rides until we came to a patch of bracken and trod it down and lay down together, close together against the chilly night; where we lay for an hour.

XIV

Caz, I said, did you hear anything? What was it? It sounded like horses' hooves on the road. Listen.

There is was again. He heard it too. We ran to a clearing and climbed on a fallen tree to see the road. In the distance there was a carriage bowling down the middle of the road; it turned out of sight under the poplars where the road turned.

It is going to the station five miles off, said Caz; I mean, its going to Hedley Halt, not the other one.

Yes, I said, but it stopped, it stopped first before it went on again.

I think I know what it is, said Caz.

I looked up at him, he looked rather pleased with himself. Well, we shall soon see.

We went back to the rectory. I was shivering.

Caz, I said, there is something terrifying about a carriage that stops at midnight and then goes on again; why is that?

We ran up the back stairs and into Heber's bedroom. Heber was there, and Tiny also, cowering on his knees by the bed.

Did you hear anything? Caz said.

Uncle was standing up looking like a lion, very stern. Yes, he said, and I hear it again.

We listened. Yes, there it is, clop, clop, cloppety clop.

Why, it is coming back, I said, the carriage is coming back again.

Heber told Tiny not to wait a minute more, but to run and stop the carriage and turn it round, and so go quickly to the station, where, if he hurried, he would catch the train.

Tiny went off like a dog, but I could not let him go like a dog, and so, running quickly after him, with Caz at my heels, came at the same time with him to the carriage.

Wait, said Tiny to the coachman, an old fellow in a doze, wait. He pulled me into the carriage with him, leaving Caz standing.

You will come back, Celia, you *will* come back?

To London, to the Ministry? Oh, yes, of course, Tiny. Lying up against the carriage cushions I snuffed the smell of ammonia, stuffing and dust. I was as sad as Tiny, and more tired. Of course I will come back, I said.

Through the window I could see where Caz was standing. He had jumped the full ditch and was lolling up against a tall gate, his face was turned to the full moon which shone in the ditchwater at his feet.

How languid you sound, said Tiny. Do not go to sleep, Celia, wake up, wake up.

'To arms, to arms, Sir Consul, Lars Porsena is here. . . .'

Tiny shuddered. Celia, be serious.

Very well then, Tiny. Next week I shall be back, I promise you. Indeed, I said coldly, why should I not? . . . how *could* I not?

I heard Heber speaking this afternoon, said Tiny hurriedly, he was speaking long-distance on the telephone to St. John, speaking to St. John at the Ministry. He was saying that you should not come back—Tiny leaned closer and whispered in my ear—that you should have a longer holiday.

I take you to mean, I said, speaking briskly against Tiny's mumble, that Uncle was suggesting—that I should never come back? Oh, Tiny, I cried in quite a different voice, did Heber say that, did he say that?

But you *will* come back?

Oh, yes, I suppose so. Yes, of course, I shall come back, I suppose.

Well, we are not really ready yet, are we? said Tiny. Not ready, I mean, to stay any longer, not yet? This happy place, he said (with a large gesture through the window) is for people who are happy and resolved and calm and loving.

You understand it very well, I said crossly. Was Tiny to prove the Daniel, and read the writing which my more sophisticated cousin could not, and I?—had not the will to?

It is not for us—not yet, said Tiny, but one day it may be for us also. Celia, you have always said that we are in exile in this world and must long for home. But Heber can accept and love also this world, and so this place is for him.

A place of happiness? I said, as also my Aunt, his sister, has her place of happiness? I sighed.

And we may have it also, I think, one day, said Tiny, but rather doubtfully.

When we have ceased to be so troublesome? I said. Yes, Tiny, that is the truth, now we are very troublesome, and we are wicked. I sighed again. We are fighting and biting, I said, against something that we wish to have, something that we must have, that is dearer to us than all the world and more precious, and we are fighting against it to destroy it. But cheer up, Tiny, it cannot be destroyed. I kissed him. Good-bye, Tiny, good-bye for the moment. To-night is a wicked night, we shall be more wicked yet, my cousin and I, it will be a wicked evening. It is a good thing that you shall not see it, my gentle Tiny. Be off now, my wise one, the train will not wait.

I jumped down from the cab.

Hurry, said Caz, and coming forward he called to the driver to drive quickly on. The old man, waking from his doze, drew the whip lightly across his horse's quarters and the cab went off at a rush.

As we came into the house again, and up the stairs past Tiny's bedroom, we saw that the door was ajar and swinging slowly on its hinge, and squeaking.

That beastly hinge, said Caz, Tuffie must find some oil for it.

There is a horrible feeling in this house to-night, I said. Why, look, Tiny's curtains are being pulled out of the window like flags.

Caz looked solemn. Respectable people don't fly flags at night. What have you been saying to Tiny?

Oh, nothing very much. Just something. Just that you and I are very conceited, just two rather superior people, you know, in a state of lordly exile (I began to laugh)— heaven-born and heaven-destined, too good by half for this poor world.

Oh, really, said Caz, oh, *really*?

When we got back to Uncle's room I went over to the bed and, lying flat upon it face downwards, began reading from my notebook, which I drew from under the pillow where I had hidden it.

Uncle said: Why do you go about so much with your cousin? Instead of lolling for ever in a negative mood, you should work and think positively, your cousin will never help you to that.

Well, said Caz rather stiffly (this sudden attack took us both by surprise, it was not like our uncle to be waspish). Well, sir, I shall not be here much longer, I am going to-morrow.

It is a pity you did not bring Raji with you, fretted our uncle.

We are a precious couple, I said, looking sideways at Heber, who was beginning to pace wrathfully. A pair of hangdogs, a survival from the fearful thirties, no good at all. I stuffed my handkerchief into my mouth, not to annoy Uncle with too much gaiety (for it was evidently for him a sad day)—Wretched woman that thou art, How thou piercest to my heart, With thy misery and graft, And thy lack of household craft.

Ha ha ha, laughed Caz.

Tee hee.

I turned face downwards on the bed and began to read aloud from my notebook from the quotations I had copied down, mostly of a melancholy nature. 'It is only,' I say, reading aloud to my uncle, and to my cousin, who is now standing in a bored attitude by the fire-place. 'It is only in glimpsing moments that we can be persuaded to entertain any objective reflections upon our hap.'

And even at such moments, said Caz, with how slight an attention.

He crossed to the window and started killing the mosquitoes.

And here, I go on, is a poem. It is called 'The Royal Dane'. It is Hamlet's father's ghost's farewell to Hamlet.

Oh heavens, said Caz.

Very well, then, you Uncle, listen. (I sing it to the tune of Sullivan's 'Of that there is no shadow of doubt, no possible probable shadow of doubt', etc.) Now is come the terrible mome, When I to my sulphureous home, Must go'ome, must go'ome.

Ha ha ha.

Tee hee.

It's 'sulphurous', said Caz, wiping his eyes.

That will do, Caz, get on with your mosquitoes. And Uncle, when I was cycling to the village yesterday to take the bottles back, I saw a health poster, and it had on it, for an advertisement you know, 'The midwife guards the mother's health'. So immediately I thought of a poem, well, it was already the first line of a poem, so I finished it, I wrote:

> The midwife guards the mother's health
> But she herself is on the shelf
> She cannot have a little child
> And that is why she looks so wild.

If you offer that to the Min. of Health, said Caz, they might pay you quite a lot not to use it.

I stole a look at Uncle. I could see from his expression that he was about to make a religious remark.

Caz, I said, you are so frivolous, so terribly frivolous. I sighed. It is something one does not care to think about.

There was silence now for some minutes as I read further in my book, and the mood of our uncle prevailed.

Uncle, I said, flattening my book at a turned-down page, here is a religious poem, it has terrible undertones, it comes straight from the black heart of the fiend of religious conviction, it might be Torquemada. It might also, I say, with a wink at Caz, be Tengal and all his Elks, ha ha, it might be the Communist Party itself. So here it is. But, first of all, it is called *A Humane Materialist at the Burning of a Heretic.* This humane person, this old-fashioned Trotskyite piece, is standing in the front row, he can smell the burning flesh of the heretic. This heretic has been very much tortured, because you see his deviationist opinions are not very clear cut, so you see, poor fellow, he has not been able to frame a confession that will fit in with what the torturers want, always what he says is not quite, as the editors say, 'what we had in mind'. So he has been trying, but he does not know what is in the torturer's minds for him to say; and on top of the torture and the terror and the exhaustion, he cannot also become a thought reader. So in the end it is no good, both sides give up, he is 'an unrepentant heretic', what is left of him, so what is left of him is now being burnt. So this humane materialist is standing in the front row. This is what he says, it is the poem:

> When shall that fuel fed fire grown fatter
> Burn to consumption and a pitter patter
> Of soft ash falling in a formless scatter
> Telling mind's death in a dump of matter.

There is a drawing of the man chained to a stake, because a rope would burn through, the chain will only become red-hot. I sighed.

My uncle now began to storm and rave at me: You are blasphemous, spoilt and evasive.

No, Uncle, I am nervy, bold and grim.

I now go on turning the pages of my notebook. Listen to this, I say, now just for one moment, Uncle, do not scold, listen. Oh, I think, this is something that must prick home to every writer that has sensibility and a desire, to establish himself. I look maliciously at Heber, I am reading it (I say) through my tears. 'And how persistent are your sallies, and at the same time what a scare you are in. You talk nonsense and are pleased with it; you say impudent things and are in continual alarm and apologizing for them. You declare that you are fond of nothing, and at the same time try to ingratiate yourself in our good opinion. You declare that you are gnashing your teeth, and at the same time you try to be witty so as to amuse us. You know that your witticisms are not witty, but you are evidently well satisfied with their literary value. You may perhaps have really suffered, but you have no respect for your own suffering. You may have sincerity, but no modesty; out of the pettiest vanity you expose your sincerity to publicity and ignominy. You doubtless mean to say something, but hide your last word through fear, because you have not the resolution to utter it, and only a cowardly impudence. You boast of consciousness, but you are not sure of your ground, for though your mind works, yet your heart is darkened and corrupt, and you cannot have a full genuine consciousness without a pure heart. And how intrusive you are, how you insist and grimace. Lies, lies, lies.'

My uncle is standing over me—Oh, my prophetic soul, my Onkelein, do not look at me like that—and I clutch my book tight and begin to laugh, for I have found a masterpiece of astringency to dust away the russo-bourgeois-pre-revolutionary cobwebs, and with them my uncle in this religious mood: 'A stupendous metamorphosis was performed in the ninth century, when, from a peaceable fisherman on the lake of Gennesareth, the apostle James was transformed into a valourous knight who charged at the head of Spanish chivalry in battles against the Moors ... the sword of a military order, assisted by the terrors of the Inquisition, was sufficient to remove every objection of profane criticism.' And again, I say, turning the pages, from the same pen, Uncle, listen: 'For it was not in *this* world that the Christians were desirous of being either useful or agreeable.'

I drop my head upon my book and begin to cry again,

for we are hobbled by past centuries and torn by the sufferings of Christ that we deride.

Caz cleans his hands on the curtains and comes and stands beside me at the other side of the bed. He said: It is like the little dog in Aldous Huxley who lifted his hind leg. It would be better perhaps to have a purely scientific education.

Oh, yes, I said, of course, about what can be observed and classified, free from the emotions, free from the past, oh, yes, no doubt. But it is nonsense, I said, this idea, it is nonsense and fear, nothing but fear and flight.

Observation, discipline and company, said my cousin, as if he were offering a plate of sandwiches, with the flag stuck on them to say what they were.

You see, said Caz to our uncle, I am a very positive fellow really.

I turned away from them. They went away, over to the window together, to have some conversation.

I lie down flat upon the bed, face downwards, my face pressed into the pillows. I have taken off my shoes, my feet are bare, I am relaxed in a sort of bitterness that is like a little death. The lipstick and the mascara have come off on the pillows, my face is washed and smudged in tears. I am despised and rejected; cut off, cast out, condemned. Ah, ah, ayee, the long high wail of the maladjusted. I grind my teeth, I slink along like a schoolgirl, my shoelaces are untied, the doors close in my face. Once when I was with Lopez in a refined teashop in Evesham, there was a poor dirty old man that came in, it was a mistake he had made, he could not know how refined this teashop was. So the rude and snooty teashop lady, she took him gingerly by the coat sleeve and drew him out again, she would not have him there at all, no, no, it would not do; the kind lady smiles upon the lady guests. The old man goes shuffling out, and from his damp nose the drips fall down, and as he goes he says: 'It's a fooking stook-oop teashop.'

Lying upon my Uncle's bed, I think: It's a fooking stook-oop world.

I look round the room, I look at the shabby rich curtains hanging down from their rusty hooks, at the worn carpets, and the tin hip-bath that has a couple of potted plants inside it, and a torn loofa glove hanging over the side and spilling the turkey towelling from its underneath. Why is there now this evil feeling in this beautiful house, why are we all at daggers drawn, now dogs at each other's throats?

Uncle, uncle, I cry.

He comes over to me as Caz goes lolling upon the mantel-piece. Caz is ill at ease, I can see that he is nervous, he wishes to disguise it.

What is it, Celia?

Speak to me, Uncle, I say, do not talk to Caz, it is sad for me, speak to me.

(I have been writing now for some time.)

This is your sermon, Uncle dear, I am writing your sermon for you, you will have to have a sermon you know. This is the sermon you were going to tell me when I was reading my poem, it is that. I laugh up at him and kiss his hand.

My uncle looks from me to my cousin, and now he says something that is rather a bit of old-fashioned upbringing rather sturdy, something *de chez Famille Fairchild.* You remember how papa found his little children fighting like dogs in the Fairchild nursery, so he set to and caned them all, to the rhythm of 'Dogs delight to bark and bite and 'tis their nature too'. And, then, in case they might miss the point of what a grand thing it is to be a Christian child instead of dumb beasts, he took the little ones out for a nice pic-nic. So where did they go, where did they go for

195

their nice treat, eh? Why, he took them a walk through the dark wood until they came to the common, and on that common stood the grey gallows tree, and hanging on the gallows tree in chains was the decaying body of the malefactor, that had gone off with half a yard of tallow cloth and got caught, the shifty muff; and got hung up for it, and was now hanging up aloft with the birds picking the flesh off him.

And let me say now, for all its harshness, better perhaps a child be brought up like this than some of the children I know who are bludgeoned by grown-up chat and 'not being talked down to', like the little boy who was always being instructed, who said, 'Mother's all right, but she will talk sex'.

So down below the gallows tree with its pretty swinging fruit sat the stern papa and his little children, that was now rather sobered up, you may guess, and sitting tight for company, and not any longer spitting at the eye and tearing at the throat, the way they had been before papa stepped in upon that nursery battlefield. So there was the slant of a look of the Fairchild-père in my uncle's eyes.

Uncle now said something that shot my cousin and me right up close together in a howl of laughter that set the shadows flying with the dust of old memory. Pronouncing simply in his lovable sober manner, our uncle said:

I hold with discipline, control, sobriety and diligence. I was myself twice flogged through Homer.

My cousin and I cannot speak for laughing, we choke and spit. *Not you, too, Uncle?* we cry. Not you too? For first there was Basil, and then there was Tom, and then there was Tiny, and then there was Caz, and now there is Uncle. Not you, too!

And surely, I said, the second time, the second time

lapping puffing-like round the Homeric course, surely this *second time* there cannot have been the same sturdy need for the goad. Why, did you for instance this second time remember nothing of the far-shooting Apollo, the war-wed, war-won, war-wakening Helene, and the tomb that Odysseus set up, the ruffianly sly robber, the cunning in council, the ess aitch number-one tee?

What tomb was that, Celia? asked Caz, prompting kindly.

The tomb that he set up above that Hecuba he murdered and tore so foully, the tomb that said in clear writing, you could read it from the sea-coast, coming up on a little sailing craft, the words that said, Kunos, KUNOS SEMA, tomb of a bitch; a bitch, a bitch, a bitch.

We go off into laughter again.

That is not in Homer, said my Uncle.

What it is, I say, to have had the education of a gentleman, with no nonsense about the science and the physics, and the boring old check-it-up and write-it-down and stick-to-what-you-see. Give me the classics all the time, and the fine old liars of historians, with their inspired imaginations working at pressure upon the stuff of dream and scandal.

And telling us, said Caz (with a slight hiccup where he had caught his breath laughing) that the Trojans were heroes who slew with chivalry, they were the British, ha, ha; but the Greeks fought like black dogs and slew foully, they were the Germans, ha, ha, the perishing blighters, the poor bleeding huns.

And all in such dreary bad verse, I said, not Homer I mean, but the Latins. What a shame that little boys should get smacked so much for such dreary and second-hand cheap thoughts as Nox est peretua una dormienda, docta puella fuit mea Lesbia. Et cetera.

Ha, ha, ha, came the echoes. The room was now getting

rather dark, the walls stood like a fortress, the moon had gone down, and the windows were black against a black sky.

Uncle now lies down flat on the bed off which I have got up to hold on to Caz.

Oh, said Caz, shivering, there is a feeling of evil in this house to-night, oh, it is the laughter and what runs in the echo, oh. He put his hands to his face.

All right, Uncle, I say, now I will read you your sermon that I have written for you, and I smooth back the papers to read. It is very religious, Uncle. Listen:

'There is little laughter where you are going and no warmth. In that landscape of harsh winter where the rivers are frozen fast, and the only sound is the crash of winter tree-branches beneath the weight of the snow that is piled on them, for the birds that might have been singing froze long ago, dropping like stone from the cold sky' (I lick my lips), 'the soul is delivered to a slow death. For in that winter landscape there is no shelter for her delicate limbs, for her soft downy and voluptuous head. On the horizon trees stand like gallows, and in the foreground of our picture—by Breughel out of Hecate—there is a wheel with studs stuck on it. What can that be? The soul, frivolous and vulnerable, will now lie down and draw the snow over her for a blanket. Now she is terrified, look, the tears freeze as they stand in her eyes. She is naked in this desert, she has no friends, she is alone. The skin of the body clothes the delicate nerves, there is no part of it that is free from pain. Racked by useless grief, for grief is useless and also insolent that is not rooted in repentance, she will now lie down and draw the snow over her. But the wind that draws from the east, blowing from the frozen tundras of Thibet and Russia, snatches away from her that *cold* covering; she is as naked as when she was born, but now there is no friendly hand to raise her up "with customary and domestic kindness". *With customary and domestic kindness.'*

I go on reading.

When I have finished reading my sermon Caz says, I was reading a book the other day about a man who jumped on the face of the dying and bragged about it to a comrade, it was in the religious wars. Well, said the comrade, it is such a terrible moment anyway, I could not do that. So I have seen it in this war, said Caz, in the fighting sometimes a man will stay with a man who is dying until he dies, he will stay beside him whether it is a friend or an enemy until he dies; he will shift him a little for comfort, or prop him up, and so he will hold him until he dies—'with customary and domestic kindness'—yes, often, when there is a lull in the fighting, I have seen this.

I tear the papers of my sermon into pieces and let the pieces fall on the floor. I say, Uncle, if men were not so positive they would be more kind. Uncle, I cry, I detest your Christianity that will be so positive. Unknown, unknown, unknown, let that be the life to come and the world that lies beyond. Uncle, if I were the Virgin Mary, I would say: No, no, I will have no part in it, no saviour, no world to come, nothing. Uncle, I say, it is George Moore's story that has the truth of it, and the pity. He said that he was taken down from the Cross and nursed back to health, and nursed back from the wounds and the sickness and the opinions, he was nursed back by Joseph's old nurse—with customary and domestic kindness—till back again he went in peace and quietness to keep his sheep and be silent.

Caz says: You are mad, Celia, you are absolutely mad, it is not Christianity that is the enemy, why nobody but the Archbishop thinks of it at all; it is the modern religions of Communism and Fascism, that is where we must look out.

Ha, ha, ha, I say, so *you* say. But the Archbishop is in the right of it, he is a very strong man, very wise, very astute. Death and the world to come will always be in men's minds, it is that they will think about, it touches their pride; they think they were not born to die.

I have a long sad pause for a moment while I am thinking that I hope so much that death is the death of the mind, and I think: Oh, beastly mind that shifts so much, that is a tyrant, that runs every way and every way at once; that will be one thing never, that will be no one thing that is not laughter, contempt and war.

But close within there sits the soul that is a crystal carapace that no claw can scratch, that has no mark upon it for all mind's storms, that feeds upon the tears and the blood. And why should it not so feed? Is it not of God? sent out to be lost for a time? to return? So let it feed and grow fat, and return to God in admirable plight, yes, let it feed.

Our Uncle now speaks to us from the bed. He is like a holy martyr lying in his agony, with death upon his lips and the final valuable word. He says that we are Christian children and yet that we are ruled by fear. He says to me: You, a Christian child, to be ruled always by fear. It is something like this; yes, this is what it is.

At these words of our uncle's, these mild and judging words, there is at once from outside the bedroom coming from behind the closed door the snicker of a suppressed laughter that will be suppressed no longer. The door opens inwards, I run across the room. It is Clem. He falls inwards upon the mat, it is Clem.

Oh dear, oh dear, he lies there in a paroxysm of laughter. He stuffs his handkerchief into his mouth, he rolls over and looks up at me. He is this horrible man, he is the most horrible man I have ever seen.

You, a Christian child—he mimics so cleverly—to be ruled always by fear. Oh dear, oh dear. Look at the Christian child, look at her mascara half-way down her cheeks, what a horrible looking girl, really at the moment you are a perfectly smudged monster. The child, the Christian child, oh dear, oh dear.

I take a flying kick at him and overbalance him and kick at his face.

Caz pulls me off. Stop it, Celia, he says, what a fool you are.

Heber gets up off the bed and stands up looking like a strong lion that is noble, that will speak. If you want to see Tiny, he says, he has gone.

Gone? says Clem, holding his handkerchief to his nose. Oh, come, how can he have gone? I passed nobody on the road, he is certainly here.

He went off in the carriage, said Uncle, and caught the last train. Are you staying?

Clem looked about him in a disagreeable way: I have your word for it he is not here?

Uncle did not say anything.

When is the next train? said Clem.

There is a train at two o'clock.

And five miles to go; I suppose I may walk?

You can have the trap.

Tuffie now comes into the room in a plaid dressing gown, she is looking rather wild. I have harnessed Caramel, she says, the trap is ready.

The expression on Clem's face is now a mixture of feebleness and ferocity. But he can do nothing. But he would like to do something. But it is his brother he is after. He looks like he would say: I will come back for you another time. But there is nothing he can do, and the train goes in an hour and a half. So off he goes.

I'll drive him, says Caz.

No, no, Caz, don't go, I say, stay here.

I'll drive him, says Tuffie, very quiet and strong.

They go off.

Stay with me, Caz, I say.

I'll go and get some blankets, he says.

Uncle darling, I say, I love you so much. I go to him and take his hand. I think, I say, that perhaps Confucius is right, perhaps he is really in the right of it, he says that human beings are our concern, and not heaven or hell or the life to come, and indeed, with human beings, yes, just with this and no more, it is already enough; Confucius says that if you return good for evil, what then will you return for good? No, he says, return rather good for good, and for evil, justice. I love you, I return good to you, do not think evil of me, do not.

He is looking happy in the flickering light, he goes and lies down on the bed and composes himself to sleep.

When Caz came back we spread the blankets on the hearthrug and lay down together.

God bless you, Celia, said our uncle, and you too Caz, and my son Tom, God bless him.

God bless us all, sir, said Caz, and took my hand in his.

Amen, I said, and fell asleep.